LABELS AND OTHER STORIES

ALSO BY LOUIS DE BERNIÈRES

POETRY

FICTION

NON-FICTION

LABELS AND OTHER STORIES

LOUIS DE BERNIÈRES

HARVILL *SECKER*
LONDON

1 3 5 7 9 10 8 6 4 2

Harvill Secker, an imprint of Vintage,
20 Vauxhall Bridge Road,
London SW1V 2SA

Harvill Secker is part of the Penguin Random House group of companies
whose addresses can be found at global.penguinrandomhouse.com

First published by Harvill Secker in 2019

A CIP catalogue record for this book is available from the British Library

penguin.co.uk/vintage

ISBN 9781911215646 (hardback)
ISBN 9781911215653 (trade paperback)

Typeset in 11/15.5 Adobe Caslon Pro
by Integra Software Services Pvt. Ltd, Pondicherry

Printed and bound in Great Britain by Clays Ltd, Elcograf S.p.A.

Penguin Random House is committed to a sustainable future for our
business, our readers and our planet. This book is made from
Forest Stewardship Council® certified paper.

LABELS AND OTHER STORIES

CONTENTS

LABELS

I was brought up in the days when there was electric light but no television, and consequently people had to learn how to amuse themselves. It was the great heyday of hobbies. People made entire villages out of matchboxes, and battleships out of matches. They made balsa aeroplanes, embroidered cassocks with coats of arms and scenes of the martyrdom of saints, and pressed flowers. My grandfather knitted his own socks, made wooden toys, cultivated friendships with spiders in his garden shed, cheated at croquet and learned how to produce his own shotgun cartridges. My grandmother's hobbies were flower-arranging and social climbing, and my mother played spirituals on the piano in between sewing new covers for the furniture and knitting woolly hats for the deserving poor. My uncle rolled his own cigars from tobacco grown and cured by himself. My other grandmother spent happy hours in the garden collecting slugs that she could drop down the grating outside the kitchen, and below a hoard of portly toads would eat them before hiding themselves once more beneath the accumulation of dead leaves.

My two sisters had a hobby called 'dressing up'. It consisted of emptying the trunks in the attic, and draping themselves in the extraordinary clothes inherited from previous generations.

caterpillars become chrysalids, made a big collection of model biplanes and Dinky cars, amassed conkers, marbles, seagull feathers and the squashy bags in the centre of golf balls. At one point I became interested in praying, and knelt quite often over the graves of our pet animals.

The morbidity of adolescence was to provide me with new joys, such as taxidermising dead animals and suffering relentless hours of torment from being agonisingly in love with several untouchable girls all at the same time. I read every Biggles book I could find, read Sir Walter Scott novels without realising that they were classics, memorised hundreds of filthy limericks and rugby songs that I can still recite faultlessly, and discovered that it was possible to have wet dreams whilst still wide awake.

Many of my friends pursued arcane hobbies, such as collecting cigarette cards and cheese wrappers, shrinking crisp packets in the oven, train and bus spotting, egg-blowing, origami, inspecting each other's endowments behind clumps of bamboo, collecting African stamps, and farming garden snails in a vivarium. One of my friends made a hobby of moles, and carved perfect representations of them in softwood with the aid of a scalpel. Another collected one hundred and fifty pairs of wings from small birds that he had shot with an air-rifle. He then suffered a crisis of conscience and joined the Royal Society for the Protection of Birds, becoming eventually one of the few people in this country to have spotted a Siberian warbler, which was unfortunately eaten by a sparrowhawk before the horrified eyes of thirteen twitchers concealed in one small hide.

Like everyone else I was reduced to extreme torpor and inactivity by the advent of television, and found that I was becoming increasingly depressed and irritable. After a couple of years I realised that I was suffering from the frustration of having no interests in life, and searched around for something to do.

I was in our corner shop one day when I was most forcibly struck by the appealing eyes of a cat depicted on the label of a tin of cat food, and it occurred to me that a comprehensive collection of cat food labels might one day be of considerable interest to historians of industry, and that to be a connoisseur of cat food labels would surely be a sufficiently rare phenomenon for me to be able to become an eminent authority in a comparatively short time. Instantly I dismissed the idea from my mind as intrinsically frivolous and absurd, and returned home.

An hour later, however, I was mocking myself at the same time as I was buying the tin with the appealing picture of the cat. With it comfortingly weighing down the pocket of my jacket on one side, I returned home once more, and eagerly lowered it into a pan of hot water so that I could soak off the label. I wrecked it completely by trying to peel it off before the glue had properly melted, and had to go out to buy another tin. This time I waited for the paper to float free of its own accord, and carefully hung it up on a line that I had stretched from a hot-water pipe in one corner of the kitchen over to a hook that I had screwed into the frame of the window. I went out to the stationer's and bought a photograph album and some of those little corner pockets. I walked restlessly about the house all evening, waiting for the label to dry, and then could not sleep all night for getting up every ten minutes to go and test it with my fingers. In the morning, my eyes itching with tiredness, I glued the label into my album, and wrote the date underneath in white ink. Afterwards I went out and bought a hairdryer and two more cans of cat food.

I was to discover that different manufacturers have different methods of securing their labels. The easiest ones to remove are those which are glued with only one blob, relying upon the rim of the can and their tight fit to keep them in place, and the worst ones are those which are stuck in place by means of large smears at every ninety degrees. On some of them the glue is so weak that one can peel it off immediately, without soaking, and others are so tenacious that they have to be immersed in white spirit. I made a comprehensive chart in order to determine at a glance the best methods of removing the labels.

I began to accumulate an embarrassment of delabelled tins, which grew unmanageable just as soon as I realised that one can obtain them in vast sizes, as well as in the smaller sizes that one commonly finds in supermarkets. I rebelled against the wasteful idea of simply throwing them away, and took to giving them away to friends who possessed cats. They were very suspicious at first, and were reluctant to give the food to their pets in case it turned out to be adulterated, or was in fact steamed pudding, or whatever. They soon came round to the idea, however, when the offerings were unspurned by their cats, as did the owners of the catteries, to whom I gave the industrial-sized cans. I did notice that many of these people were beginning to look at me askance, as though I was a little mad, and it is the truth that I stopped receiving invitations to dinner parties because my conversation had become monomaniac. I think the worst thing was when my wife left me, saying that she would not consider coming back until I had removed all the albums from her side of the bedroom. The house became a terrible tip because I had had no experience of doing the housework, and eventually I had to pay her to come back once a week in order to dust and tidy.

It occurred to me that the easiest way of obtaining labels would be to write to pet food companies and request samples, past and present, but I received no cooperation at all. My first reply was similar to all the others, and ran like this:

Dear Sir,

Our manager asks me to thank you for your kind letter, and assures you that it is receiving his closest attention.

With best wishes to you and your pussy, we remain, yours sincerely ...

Having received this letter, I would hear nothing more.

It may surprise many people to know that the variety of cat food labels is virtually infinite. To begin with, every manufacturer changes the label fairly frequently in order to modify the targeting of the customer, and to attempt to gain an edge over other brands. Thus a brunette might be changed to a blonde to make a particular food more glamorous, and a Persian cat might be substituted for a ginger moggy in order to give an impression of high class. Shortly afterwards the woman might be changed to a beautiful Asian in order to appeal to the burgeoning immigrant market, and the cat be changed to a tabby to give it a no-nonsense, no-woofers-around-here, working-class appeal. The labels are often changed by the addition of 'special offer' announcements, or, most annoyingly, by 'free competitions' where the competition is on the back of the label so that one has to buy two cans the same in order to have both the obverse and the front in one's album.

In addition, every supermarket has its own brand, and every manufacturer is constantly adding to the range, so that whereas in the old days there was just Felix, Whiskas, Top Cat, etc., each one now has flavours such as rabbit and tuna, quail, salmon, pigeon, truffles and calf liver, each one with different labels as detailed above. Everyone knows that the food is mostly made of whales slaughtered by the Japanese for 'scientific research', cereals, French horses, exhausted donkeys and bits of the anatomy of animals that most people would prefer not to eat, but recently the producers have cottoned on to the fact that cat owners tend to buy the food that their cat likes the most, and consequently have introduced greater and greater quantities of finer meat, so that indeed one finds real pieces of liver and genuine lumps of rabbit.

It was when my collection began to go international that I hit the financial rocks. I had been working for several years as a bailiff, a job to which I was well suited on account of my great size and my ability to adopt an intimidating expression. I had managed to remain afloat by cutting expenses wherever possible: my house was falling apart, my garden was a wilderness, my car was ancient, I had bought no new clothes for five years, and I cut my own hair with the kitchen scissors. I once sat down with my albums and worked out that I had spent the equivalent of two years' salary on cat food. But I was not broke.

What brought everything to a crisis was a trip to France in pursuit of a debt defaulter. I stopped off in a Champion supermarket, and, whilst looking for a tin of cassoulet, I happened upon rows and rows of cat food with beautiful labels, many of them in black, with distinguished scrolly writing upon them. It was love at first sight, and I bought every single type I could find, not just there, but in each Mamouth and Leclerc supermarket that I passed. I found it most touching that the French have many brands that include petit pois and extra-fine haricots verts, revealing that French owners anthropomorphically impute to their cats a certain gastronomic delicacy and discrimination equivalent to their own. By misfortune I broke the back axle on the way home, and my hoard of tins eventually arrived by courtesy of the Automobile Association's relay service.

Naturally things became worse and more disastrous by the month. I made frequent weekend trips to France, and returned burdened with cans of Luxochat, Orphée, Poupouche and Minette Contente. Thereafter I took sick leave from work and discovered the treasure trove of Spain. Not for me the Alhambra; it was Señorito Gatito, Minino, Micho Miau and Ronroneo.

I came home bursting with happiness and joie de vivre, planning to cover Germany, and found that my world had fallen apart. My skiving had been discovered, and I was fired from my job, at exactly the same time that I received final demands for the electricity, the gas, the telephone and a reminder to pay my television licence. I sat amongst my albums and my pile of Spanish cans, and realised that I had allowed myself to drift into disaster. I beat myself about the head, first with my hands, and then with a rolled-up newspaper. I raised my eyes to the heavens in exasperation, moaned, rocked upon my haunches and smashed a dinner plate on the kitchen floor. Then, pulling myself together, I made an irrevocable decision to destroy my entire collection.

Out in the garden I built a sizeable bonfire from garden waste, my old deckchairs and the novelty lingerie that I had presented to my wife at birthdays and Christmases, but which she had left behind, and went indoors to collect the albums.

I found myself flicking through them. I thought, 'Well, I might just keep that one, it's the only Chinese one I've got,' and, 'I'll not throw that one away, it's a Whiskas blue from ten years ago,' or, 'That was the last one I got before my wife left. It has sentimental value.' Needless to say, I didn't burn any of them; I just got on with soaking off the labels on the Spanish cans.

My unemployment benefit did not even begin to cover my personal expenses as well as the cost of acquiring new tins, and I was reduced to buying stale loaves from the baker, and butcher's bones with which to make broth. I had to slice the bread with a saw, and would attempt to extract the marrow from the bones with a large Victorian corkscrew. I became demented with hunger, and the weight fell off me at a rate equalled only by the precipitate loss of my hair from extreme worry. One day, in desperation, I opened one of my tins, sniffed the meat, and began to reason with myself.

'It's been sterilised,' I said to myself, 'and a vet told me that it's treated to a higher standard than human food. OK, so it's full of ground testicles, lips, udders, intestines and vulvas, but so are sausages, and you like them. And what about those pork pies that are full of white bits and taste of gunpowder? They don't taste of pork, that's for sure. Besides,' I continued, 'cats are notoriously fussy and dainty eaters, apart from when they eat raw birds complete with feathers, and so if a cat finds this acceptable and even importunes people for it, maybe it's pretty nice.'

I fetched a teaspoon, and dipped the very tip of it into the meat. I raised it to my nose and sniffed. In truth it smelled quite enticing. I forced myself to place the spoon in my mouth, conquered the urge to retch, and squashed the little lump against my palate. I chewed slowly, and then ran to the sink and spat it out, overwhelmed with disgust. I sat down, consumed with a kind of sorrowful self-hatred, and began to suffer that romantic longing for death that I had not felt since I was a teenager. My life passed before my eyes, and I had exactly the same kind of melancholy reflections about the futility and meaninglessness of existence as I had experienced after Susan Borrowdale refused to go to the cinema with me, and my sister came instead because she felt sorry for me.

But these cogitations were interrupted by a very pleasant aftertaste in my mouth, and by the fact that I was salivating copiously. I picked up the can at my feet, and sniffed it again. 'All it needs,' I said to myself, 'is a touch of garlic, a few herbs, and it would really make a very respectable terrine.'

I took it into the kitchen and emptied it out into a dish. I peeled three cloves of garlic and crushed them. I grated some fresh black pepper and some herbes de Provence, and mashed the meat with the extra ingredients. I squashed it all into a bowl, levelled it off with a fork, decorated it with three bay leaves, and poured melted butter over it so that it would look like the real thing when it came out of the fridge.

It was absolutely delicious spread over thin toasted slices of stale bread; it was positively a spiritual experience. It was the gastronomic equivalent of making love for the first time to someone that one has pursued for years.

I suffered the indignity of being visited by the same firm of bailiffs for which I used to work, but my old mates were kind to me and took only things that I did not need very much, such as the grandfather clock and my ex-wife's Turkish carpet. They left me my fridge, my cooker, my collection of books on the manufacture of terrines and pâtés, my vast accumulation of garlic crushers, peppermills, herbs and French cast-iron cookware. I feel I should explain that I never could do things by halves; I always have to possess complete collections.

I became extremely good at my new vocation. The more expensive cat foods made exquisite coarse pâtés and meat pies (my shortcrust pastry is quite excellent, and I never leave big gaps filled up with gelatine, as most pie-makers do). The cheaper ones that have a lot of cereal generally do not taste very good unless they are considerably modified by the addition of, for example, diced mushroom and chicken livers fried in olive oil. Turkey livers are a little too strong and leave a slightly unpleasant aftertaste.

The fish-based cat foods are generally very hard to use. With the exception of the tuna and salmon, they always carry the unmistakable aroma of cat food, which is caused, I think, by the overuse of preservatives and flavour-enhancers. They are also conducive to lingering and intractable halitosis, as any owner of an affectionate cat will be able to confirm.

And so this is how cat food, which got me into so much trouble, also got me out of it. I began by supplying the local delicatessen, and was surprised to find that I was able to make over one hundred per cent profit. I redoubled my efforts, and learned to decorate my products with parsley and little slices of orange. I learned the discreet use of paprika, and even asafoetida. This spice smells of cat ordure, but is capable of replacing garlic in some recipes, and in that respect it is similar to parmesan cheese, which, as everyone knows, smells of vomit but improves the taste of minced meat.

I also discovered that the addition of seven-star Greek brandy is an absolute winner, and this led me on to experiments with calvados, Irish whiskey, kirsch, Armagnac, and all sorts of strange liquors from Eastern Europe and Scandinavia.

But what really made the difference was printing the labels in French, which enabled me to begin to supply all the really expensive establishments in London; *'Terrine de Lapin à l'Ail'* sounds far more sophisticated than 'Rabbit with Garlic', after all. I had some beautiful labels printed out, in black, with scrolly writing.

I have become very well off, despite being a one-man operation working out of my own kitchen, and I am very contented. I have outlets in delicatessens and restaurants all over Britain and one in Paris, and my products have even passed quality inspections by the Ministry of Agriculture, Fisheries and Food. It might be of interest to people to know that my only complete failure was a duck pâté that was not made of cat food at all.

I go out quite often on trips across Europe, looking for superior brands of cat food with nice labels, and my ex-wife comes with me, having moved back in as soon as I became successful. She is now most skilful at soaking off labels, and is a deft hand with an hachoir. The liver with chives was entirely her own invention, and she grows most of our herbs herself.

I recently received two letters which greatly amused me. One was from a woman in Bath who told me that my terrines are 'simply divine' and that her blue-point Persian pussycat 'absolutely adores them' as well.

The other was from a man who said that he was beginning a collection of my 'most aesthetically pleasing' labels, and did I have any copies of past designs that I could send to him? I wrote back as follows:

Dear Sir,

Our manager thanks you for your letter and asks me to assure you that it is receiving his closest attention.

Naturally I never wrote back again, nor did I send him any labels. Nonetheless, I feel a little sorry for him, and anxious on his behalf; it's easy enough to turn cat food into something nice, but what do you do with hundreds of jars of pâté? With him in mind, I had a whole new range of labels printed in fresh designs, with details of a competition on the reverse.

GÜNTER WEBER'S CONFESSION

It is not entirely true that Leutnant Günter Weber stayed away from the doctor's house after the massacre of the Italian soldiers. He came back once, very briefly, seven months afterwards, in the spring.

He paused at the entrance to the yard and ran his fingers over the table where Pelagia used to cut up onions, and where the boys of La Scala used to drink robola together and sing. With the tip of his jackboot he nudged the frayed end of the rope that formerly attached Pelagia's goat to the olive tree. He sniffed the air, and took his cap off and on several times, because he was unsure whether or not to wear it, and because he needed a pretext for wasting a little time. He thought of leaving, but then summoned up his courage and tapped on the door.

When Pelagia answered it, an expression of such fear and horror passed over her face that Weber felt as if someone had driven a long pin into his heart. 'Please, signora,' he said, in Italian, 'don't be afraid. I'm alone, and I need to see your father.'

'He's not here,' said Pelagia desperately.

Weber sighed and turned his head away, as if to look at the view. 'I know he's here. I saw him come in. Please, I mean no harm. I have come to tell him something very important.'

They looked at each other. She saw that he had heavy rings under his eyes, as if he had given up sleep for ever, and his complexion had become sallow, like that of a heavy smoker. He was still striking and somewhat handsome, but the youth and eagerness had gone out of his bearing even though he was only twenty-three years old, as if all his pride had evaporated. He looked at Pelagia, and regretted that her prettiness and vivacity had been devoured so unpityingly by the war. She was too thin, and he could almost scent her terror, as though she had bathed in it for months.

'You are still beautiful,' he lied, attempting the gallantry that he not quite managed to learn from the Italians.

Pelagia twisted her mouth sceptically, barely able to disguise her anger. 'Your people beat my father up,' she said suddenly, 'and they smashed all his medical equipment. And they stubbed out cigarettes on Drosoula's breasts.'

'Don't accuse me,' said Weber, 'it wasn't me.' She looked back at him in silence, telling him that he was one of them. 'I need to see your father,' he repeated.

'Do you remember the little animal we had?' persisted Pelagia.

'The pine marten? Psipsina?'

'Your people killed her as well.' Pelagia knew that it was unwise to be indignant with a Nazi officer, even a former friend, but she had too much anger and grief buried alive inside her. Like one entombed by an avalanche, it tried to claw its way out even as it suffocated for want of air and light.

'I need to see your father,' repeated Günter Weber.

'I am here,' said Dr Iannis, appearing behind his daughter and placing his hand upon her shoulder. The beating he had endured and the destruction of his lifetime's collection of medical instruments had left him diminished. One lens of his spectacles was broken, with no prospect of replacement. He tried to wear them with dignity, and his brain had accustomed itself to ignoring the strange distortions that he perceived, but the effect was still sad and ludicrous. Like his daughter, he seemed to have aged rapidly in the passage of only a few months.

'It's important that I talk to you,' said Leutnant Weber, 'I have important information.'

'Important to whom?' demanded the doctor.

Weber tried to remain patient. 'You are a historian. I remember that you were trying to write a history of Cephalonia. I have information that is important to the truth.'

'Ah, the truth,' echoed the doctor ironically.

'Dr Iannis,' said Weber, his voice quite suddenly becoming a little hysterical, 'if you refuse to listen to me, I will draw my pistol and force you to. I have nothing to lose. I've had enough.' Weber's mouth twisted. 'I can't take much more of this.'

There was such pain in the young officer's voice that Dr Iannis took pity on him. He turned to his daughter, saying, '*Koritsaki mou*, go and make us some mountain tea.' He turned to Weber. 'I can't offer you coffee, as you know, and there's no food. I won't tell you what we've been living off. We gather mountain tea on the hillsides; it's the best I can offer you.'

Weber sat down heavily at the table in the yard, and placed his cap on it. He sighed, saying, 'The island is very beautiful at this time of year. I've never seen so many flowers.'

'The island has been profaned,' said the doctor curtly.

'Doctor,' said Weber, 'I want to confess to you. Let me speak.'

'Confess?' repeated the doctor, sitting down opposite him.

'This is where we sang songs and drank,' said Weber, 'the boys of La Scala, and Captain Antonio. They were the best days of my life. All gone. Sometimes I dream that I hear Antonio playing the mandolin. Do you remember that in La Scala we didn't have military ranks? I was a bad singer so my rank was "dotted demi-semiquaver rest". That was Antonio's sense of humour.'

'Is this a confession?' asked the doctor. 'Have you come here to be nostalgic about everything that you destroyed, and everyone you killed?'

'I tried to get out of it,' said Weber, 'I tried to refuse to command a firing squad. They wouldn't let me. The major said that I could be shot for refusing to obey an order. He said the Italians would all be shot anyway, whether I refused or not. I think,' he said, 'that you should realise that not all of us are without a conscience.'

'Are you asking me to feel sorry for you?' demanded the doctor.

Weber looked at him desperately. 'The order came from the Führer.' The doctor returned his gaze, and saw the tears well up in Weber's eyes. The young German blurted out, 'It was me. It was me who commanded the squad. I had to shoot my own friends. Carlo, and Antonio, all the boys.'

Dr Iannis felt his throat go dry.

Weber continued, 'Antonio was behind Carlo. He didn't die straight away. When I went to give the coup de grâce, I bent down, and Antonio's eyes looked straight back. I was going to finish him off, but I couldn't.' Weber hung his head, his voice growing weak and pitiful. 'That was all I could do to salvage some honour, letting Antonio die more slowly.'

The doctor kept his peace. Part of him would have loved to have told Weber that Antonio Corelli had been dragged from beneath the heap of bodies, and that he had lived, but he knew that it was dangerous to tell such things even to a German who had almost been a friend.

'As long as I live,' said Weber, 'I'll never forget Antonio's face, all scarlet with blood. And those eyes, looking back at me, all glowing, and full of tranquillity.'

Pelagia came out bearing a tray with two small cups of pale yellow liquid. She placed them before Weber and Dr Iannis, and retreated without saying a word.

'I already knew it was you,' said the doctor, adding hurriedly, 'Word gets around in such a small place.' He leaned forward, cupping the glass of tea in his hands. 'And I'll tell you something else.' He paused. 'I looked at some of the bodies you left lying around before you disposed of them. I looked at the bodies of the Italian officers that were thrown in that pit near the lighthouse, and you know what? Your firing squads were shooting them in the legs so that it wouldn't be them who were the murderers. They shot them in the legs so that you officers would have to finish them off with a shot in the head, and be the true assassins. Did you know that? That's how your soldiers kept themselves innocent.'

Weber sat absolutely still. He closed his eyes, and muttered, 'My God, my God.'

'So now you've confessed,' said the doctor.

'No,' replied Weber, 'I haven't. I came to tell you something else. I just wanted to tell you about Antonio and the boys first. It's a double confession, perhaps.'

The doctor remained wordless, knowing that Weber would talk without prompting, given sufficient time. 'I ... ' began the young man, and then he choked. He put his head in his hands and blurted out, 'Two weeks ago I had to kill a woman.'

'There is no chivalry here,' said the doctor, waving his right hand, as if to indicate the island, its suffering, its long history, its occupation by barbarians from the north. 'Why is it so bad to kill a woman when you have killed so many men? Isn't a life a life?'

'I've never killed a woman,' said Günter Weber, 'but now I've had to. I just couldn't stand to hear her screaming any more.'

'Tell me,' said the doctor, who was longing to light his pipe, but had had nothing to smoke in it for days.

'It's the communists,' explained Weber.

'The communists?'

'The KKE. We kill communists. It's our policy. We go into a village, we get everyone out in the plaza, and we say "Who are the communists?" and if anyone is pointed out, we kill them straight away. We hang them on the plane trees.'

'I know all this,' said the doctor, his voice unmistakably betraying his anger and disgust.

'Two weeks ago I was in such a village, and a woman was pointed out by another villager, so we had to get the rope ready. We slung it over a branch, and then the woman went crazy. It's hard for me to tell you. It's so hard, Doctor.'

'Well?' said Dr Iannis.

'She started to scream and wail. She threw herself down and writhed in the dust. Her eyes were rolling. And she crawled through the dirt and threw her arms about my knees, and she was crying, "*Eleos, eleos, eleos. Eimai athoa, eimai athoa.*" I don't know what it means, but I can't forget it, I hear it every moment, that wild voice, terrified, screaming, "*Eleos, eleos. Eimai athoa, eimai athoa.*"'

standing around, you could see that some of the men were getting to the point where they were thinking of attacking us, because they couldn't stand it any longer either, all that writhing and howling, and the women of the village started to join in the howling as well, and then suddenly I decided to have mercy on the woman, and not hang her after all.'

'You spared her?'

'When she was eating dirt and choking on it, I drew my pistol and shot her through the back of the head.'

'This is mercy?' demanded the doctor quietly.

'I had to put her out of her misery.'

'No,' said the doctor, 'you had to put yourself out of her misery.'

'Believe me, it was mercy,' said Weber. 'You weren't there. It was mercy.'

'Do you have any cigarettes?' asked Dr Iannis. 'I don't normally smoke them, but I have nothing any more.'

Weber produced a silver cigarette case and flipped it open. The doctor flagrantly took two cigarettes, and reached into the pocket of his jacket. He took out his pipe and broke the cigarettes into it, slowly and lovingly packing the tobacco down. Weber offered him a petrol lighter, and the doctor sucked the smoke in deeply. He exhaled, saying, 'The first taste after a long break is always the best, and then later it turns bitter, and you wonder how you ever began a habit so abominably vile.'

The doctor considered his thoughts, ordered them, and then told Weber, 'Young man, everyone knows all the news on this island. It is small and intimate. Everyone knows everyone else, more or less. The woman you killed was Julia Galiatsatos. I heard about it.'

'Yes?' asked Weber, as if inviting the doctor to continue.

'I didn't know it was you who killed her, though. She comes from a family that has been royalist ever since the first king arrived. I often disputed with her father, when he was alive, because I am a Venizelist, if that means anything to you.'

Weber shrugged, and the doctor pursued his point. 'In other words she was the very opposite of a communist. The man who pointed her out as a communist was her cousin, who would inherit her property in the event of her death. They despised each other heartily, and quarrelled frequently. It was both a scandal and a joke to everyone in the area.'

Weber was speechless. Dr Iannis nodded slowly. 'Yes, young man, it was a question of spite and of greed. As I said, there are no communists to speak of. There are, however, a number of people that I would not exactly describe as having inherited the Hellenic frame of mind. Regrettably, we have some people here who are venal, unprincipled and delinquent. Every time you kill a "communist" you are in fact doing the dirty work of a relative, or you are helping someone out with a vendetta. It apparently never occurs to Germans that they might be made fools of. That is certainly my observation.'

Weber's face twisted. 'I'm going to go back there,' he said, his voice bilious with disgust. 'I'm going to find that son of a bitch and kill him with my own hands.'

'Too late,' said Dr Iannis, shaking his head mockingly. 'There were those who were ashamed of what had been done. The man who accused Julia Galiatsatos is now under the ground with his skull in fragments. I attended the case, and I was not overly sorry to lose the patient.' The doctor tapped the dottle out of his pipe and looked very levelly at the leutnant. 'You've

been here how long? And you still don't understand us at all,
do you? You see us, and our image makes no more impression
on your retina than the shadow of a ghost; you hear us, and our
words bounce off your brain like an olive falling to the ground.
All you listen to are the half-baked, monstrous and monoton-
ous oversimplifications that are born of your own ignorance.'

Weber was on the point of rising to his feet and command-
ing 'That's enough, Doctor', but he restrained himself. His
sorrow and remorse had acquired an appalling taste of worm-
wood. He wondered whether he would ever be able to cleanse
the war from his memory and imagination. He struggled with
a steadily growing conviction that he had accidentally become
estranged to the common purpose of mankind, that he had
taken an inviting fork in the path that had led first to thorns,
and then to an abyss.

'So you killed a woman,' added the doctor, 'and you came
here to confess. Why don't you confess to a priest? You are a
Catholic, I presume.'

Weber took something from his pocket. It was a small
smoked sausage from Bavaria. He laid it on the table without
saying anything about it, as though the action were not his own.
He looked up at the doctor, his mouth working, his face wan
with tiredness and self-contempt. 'I am a Lutheran, but I went
to a priest anyway.' He looked away, and added, 'It is sometimes
not enough to confess to a priest.'

Weber stood and replaced his cap on his head. He squared
his shoulders, briefly resembling the proud young grenadier he
had once been. He stood to attention and saluted the doctor. It
was not the Hitler salute, but the military one that had been in
use before, and which was now forbidden. The doctor did not

respond, unsure in any case of what might constitute a suitable response. Weber let his hand drop to his side, and he walked stiffly and self-consciously to the entrance of the yard, where he turned to look around it for the last time. He nodded to the doctor, and without another word he left.

Pelagia came out as soon as he had gone. She went to the table and picked up the sausage. Her mouth watered almost uncontrollably, the hunger whelming up so strongly from her entrails so that she felt faint, and had to sit down.

'I suppose you heard all that,' said Dr Iannis.

Pelagia nodded her head, and, holding up the sausage, asked, 'What shall we do with this?'

Both she and her father remembered how Antonio and the other Italians had used to bring them food that they had stolen from their own field kitchens and messes, and they fell silent for a moment. The doctor suppressed the salivation in his own mouth that was threatening to make speech impossible, and said as disinterestedly as he could, 'You eat it, *koritsaki mou*. You're young, you need the protein more than I do.'

'You have it,' she said, offering it to him.

'Really, I couldn't. I'm not hungry.'

Pelagia understood the generosity and necessity of her father's lie, and she put the sausage back on the table. 'I'm not hungry either,' she said.

Later that evening, after they had dined on the roasted corms of spring flowers, Pelagia came out into the yard and picked up the sausage. She sniffed it, and was tempted to bite into it. Instead she went out into the village and walked about with it distractedly until finally she gave it to an emaciated dog, one of the fortunate ones that had not yet been eaten.

THE TURKS ARE SO WONDERFUL WITH CHILDREN

Robert and Susan Freeman were perfectly cut out for one another. For one thing, they were both only children, whose parents had died when they were young. Robert's had perished in a boating accident in the Lake District, and Susan's had died separately, a year apart, each of cancer. Both Robert and Susan had been brought up by elderly relatives, and had no one left in the world by the time they were in their early twenties, so that when they met on the same Public Administration course at university, it seemed rather wonderful to have so much in common, and it was almost inevitable that they should forge a bond.

If they fell in love with each other at university, it was immediately afterwards that they fell for Turkey, in the year before they were married, when they were taking that crucial first holiday together, the one wherein people discover whether or not their relationship really has any future. They had not only fallen even more in love with each other, but had also become enamoured of the country itself, which had turned out to be quite different from their expectation. They had gone there in some trepidation, expecting to encounter the slavering rapists, torturers and assassins of popular European myth, only to find a humorous, honest, hospitable, polite and affectionate people with a marvellous cuisine, whose main fault was a tendency to expound their opinions at extraordinary length and with many repetitions of the same point. You couldn't win an argument with a Turk because you were filibustered, and so Susan and Robert sedulously avoided all political discussion.

Robert and Susan enjoyed the way in which Turks employ their tractors as a kind of family car, idling along with a trailer-load of relatives, and they enjoyed the slow chaos of Turkish life in general, but what appealed to them in particular, on that idyllic first holiday together, was that the Turks were so kind to animals. Our couple were unashamedly soft-hearted about animals, and this kindness was such a relief after previous experiences in other countries. Robert had once been to a place in Greece where there was a dejected three-legged dog, which the locals had named 'Ecevit' so they could kick it every time it came limping up to beg for food. He had, too, been shocked by the pitiable state of the stray cats, as visitors to Greece always are. Susan, on the other hand, had once been to Italy to visit a friend with a palazzo in the Tuscan countryside, who had a well-loved but sick rabbit that the vet had refused to treat, on the grounds that it was not a proper animal. He had then offered her his mother's recipe for *coniglio al forno*. She had seen a bullfight on Spanish television once, watching it with fascinated horror through the fingers that she clamped over her eyes, and had never been back to Spain again.

The Turks, however, were surrounded by clean, sociable, trusting, well-fed, contented dogs and cats, and they even erected wire cages on the beaches, to protect the nests of turtle eggs. On Calis beach there were comical men on bicycles with enormous vernier calipers who measured the colossal creatures when they struggled ashore, grunting extravagantly like wrestlers as they attempted to turn them over and tag them. In short, it was pleasant to go to a place where the folk were as sweet-willed towards animals as most of the British are. When he was feeling sententious Robert liked to say, 'The real index of civilisation is when people are kinder than they need to be,' and by this reckoning the Turks were civilised indeed.

It was when they were blessed with a child, however, that they realised that the Turks were also wonderful with children, and this became the true reason for their repeated return.

Little Vinnie arrived in the third year of their marriage, and to begin with he had been a perfectly normal baby, which is to say that he had yelled, excreted and slept. He did, however, gnaw at Susan's nipples as if he were a dog at a bone, and she had soon been obliged to change over to a bottle, whose teat had regularly to be replaced. It was as soon as he could crawl that it was fully borne in upon them that their child was going to be difficult. Screaming with pleasure, he took to throwing himself on the family cats, grasping handfuls of their flesh, and wrenching it. One by one the animals suffered the equivalent of a feline nervous breakdown, and lost all sense of bladder control. All three of them left home in the same week to find themselves alternative accommodation, where their equanimity was ultimately restored. Vinnie began a similar campaign against the dog, so that, as soon as he crawled near, the persecuted animal would have to spring to his feet and flee to another room. Robert and Susan assured themselves that Vinnie would soon grow out of it, that he was, after all, only a child, but already they felt distinctly uneasy.

When he could toddle, Vinnie learned the delights of switching off essential electrical appliances. He turned off the fridge several times, so that occasionally the kitchen was flooded on account of the unplanned defrosting, and once he turned off the deep freeze just a day after Robert had returned from a superstore with a month's supply of meat. When Susan opened the lid a week later, she beheld a monstrous heaving of maggots, and a sordid flood of brown, green and yellow slime. Seconds later, a smell from the vilest imaginings of Satan assaulted her nostrils, and she fell backwards and fainted, burying herself beneath a cascade of tin cans, rice and jam jars.

When he began to talk, Vinnie destroyed Susan's and Robert's social life. It is, of course, an invariant law of nature that children cripple their parents' social life, as well as their sex life, and indeed any other kind of life they may be attempting to lead, but Vinnie went far beyond the point of mere disablement. He did not merely cripple it, he literally destroyed it.

It began with the telephone. It would ring and Vinnie would pick it up, say 'Goodbye' in his childish treble, and put the phone back on the hook. The phone would ring again, and the caller would say 'Vinnie, is your mother there?' and the boy would say 'Yes,' and put the phone back on the hook. It would ring once more, and the agitated voice would go 'Vinnie, please go and fetch your mother, I've got to speak to her,' whereupon Vinnie would put the phone back on the hook and fetch his mother, who would come to the phone only to find the receiver in place, and nobody on the other end of the line.

It continued with Vinnie's treatment of callers who arrived at the house. He was normally very clean, but if there was a visitor, that was when he chose to do both kinds of business in the middle of the kitchen floor. Vinnie liked to creep up behind the sofa and pull the hair of any woman who happened to be lounging on it. If anyone was a smoker, Vinnie would appropriate their lighter and try to set fire to the coats and scarves that they had left hanging on the pegs in the hallway. If anyone brought their little girls, Vinnie would prise their dolls away from them, and twist off their heads. He would take worms, earwigs and woodlice from the garden, and pop them into the mouths of babies, and he taught himself how to let down the tyres of cars as they stood in the driveway outside.

As his verbal abilities improved, it emerged that he had a strong streak of psychological cruelty. To women he would say things like 'Why are you so ugly?', and he once announced to a very venerable and frail gentleman that 'I expect you're going to die quite soon, aren't you?' When his interlocutor bravely assented to this proposition, Vinnie just said, 'I expect we'll all be glad, won't we?'

Susan and Robert suffered their child for four years before they took him to see a child psychiatrist.

Dr Pedicue had a room in a social services centre. It was filled with comforting and pleasant things, such as a goldfish tank, building blocks, mechanical toys, teddy bears and child-sized chairs. He was a patient man who had encountered many a demented and many a haunted child, and on the first visit he sent Robert and Susan away whilst he performed the normal developmental tests for intelligence and spatial reasoning. Vinnie came out slightly above average, but when the parents returned they found the doctor nursing a terrible bruise on his forehead. Vinnie had knotted his shoelaces together, and he had taken a fall, cracking his head on the edge of a desk. The most sinister thing was that Vinnie had apparently not laughed. He had smiled, complacently.

The next time, Vinnie took the tests for manual dexterity and verbal ability. When his parents came back, they found Dr Pedicue, grim-faced, sitting behind his desk, with two shiny red objects laid out on the blotting paper in front of him.

'How did Vinnie do?' asked Susan innocently, and Dr Pedicue motioned to the two objects in front of him. 'He scores well for manual dexterity,' said the doctor. 'Look at that; I was only out of the room for a few seconds.'

Susan and Robert looked down at the two dead goldfish. Each one had had a biro inserted into its mouth and jammed down its throat as far as it would go.

'I can't find anything wrong with your son,' said Dr Pedicue, after four more visits. 'I mean, there's nothing technically wrong with him that I can find. I can't give you a diagnosis.' He paused for thought, wondering whether or not it was wise to continue, until finally he said, 'May I speak off the record?'

Susan and Robert nodded, rightly anticipating the very worst. 'Sometimes we get appalling parents who produce absolutely faultless and wonderful children,' the doctor told them, 'and sometimes we get perfect parents who produce children so awful that they ought to be subjected to euthanasia before they inflict irreparable damage on the human race. I can't explain this. I mean, usually it's awful parents who have awful children, but sometimes you get these inexplicable exceptions. Your child is one of these.'

'Can't you do anything then?' asked Susan fearfully.

'If I can't diagnose, I can't treat,' said the doctor, raising his hands in a gesture of defeat. 'I mean, your child is obnoxious and malevolent. He's evil, and that isn't a condition I can look up in my manual.' The doctor leaned forward. 'Between you and me, and I hope you won't take offence, I know this isn't very professional, but your Vinnie is just a gobshite. He's a snake-in-the-grass. That's the only diagnosis I can give. All I can do is offer you my sympathy.'

Susan and Robert hung their heads, and Dr Pedicue went over to the window and stood there for a few moments with his hands behind his back. Then he turned and said, 'I don't know if you're Catholic or not, but if you are, you might try exorcism. I think that in your situation I would be desperate enough to try it. And I'm an agnostic.'

Vinnie's parents grew more dejected and despondent by the day. They had no friends left; cautionary word had spread amid the local coterie of babysitters and, in rotation, the nursery schools of the area had resorted to expulsion, so that there was no prospect of a moment's peace at home. Susan gave up her job because Robert's was better paid, and they sold her car in order to make ends meet. Her life became a dismal succession of torments, incarcerated as she was, with a diminutive but endlessly inventive demoniac.

One evening, as she was getting ready for bed, Susan sat in front of the mirror at her dressing table and realised what Vinnie had done to her. Her skin was lined and sallow, her cheeks were sunken, there were black hollows under her eyes, her cracked lips twitched at the corners, and her thick black hair had thinned and greyed. Her hairbrush removed generous tufts with every stroke. Suddenly she put her hands to her face and began to sob. Robert came up behind her and placed a trembling hand on her shoulder. After some minutes, when her tears had subsided, she said, 'He's my child, and I can't love him. Oh Robbie, I just want to kill him. I can't bear it any longer, really I can't.'

'We'll take him to Turkey,' said Robert. 'This is a window of opportunity, if you think about it. We can do what we've been talking about. It's probably now or never.'

Turkey was the only place where Vinnie began to resemble a normal human being, and Robert and Susan had often wondered why. Vinnie was quite a pretty child, with his mother's creamy white skin, black hair and dark brown eyes, and in Turkey he was for most of the time firmly clamped in the arms of a succession of affectionate Turks. Robert and Susan had a theory that Vinnie was slightly frightened by the men, with their aroma of lemon cologne, their dark-roast skins and exuberant moustaches, their extraordinary toughness and physical strength, their pungent cigarettes, and their tea-stained teeth. Seized by one of these men, hugged to within an inch of his life, his hair ruffled into a mop, Vinnie would subside into something like the resemblance of a natural little boy. The women, thought Susan, confused Vinnie rather than intimidated him. Marriage turns Turkish women into something broad-backsided and formidable, but they have rather sweet round faces framed by the customary headscarf, and any stranger's child within convenient reach is perched on a sturdy hip in order to have its face crammed with lokma, lokum and baklava. 'The Turks are so wonderful with children,' sighed Robert and Susan, every time they went there, amazed by how tractable Vinnie would become.

It might have seemed strange, had they told anyone, that Robert and Susan should have decided to take a trip to south-west Turkey in July, when it was unbearably hot and bona fide connoisseurs stay away on account of the tourists, and when, to cap it all, they were in the middle of moving house from East Anglia to Cornwall. It might also have seemed strange that they were landing at Izmir airport rather than the one at Dalaman, when they were ultimately headed for Fethiye. They had their reasons, however, and their main concern was simply to reach Fethiye by Tuesday morning. Besides, some of the landscape on that long drive was absolutely wonderful. Often you came upon bands of nomads in their goatskin tents, weaving carpets on looms that they set up outdoors, and sometimes you still saw working camels, with azure prayer beads hanging from their halters. You might come round a bend on the road and see before you a view so stunning that you just had to stop for a while and look at it, even if your darling child was kicking your seat, or blowing his nose into his fingers and trying to smear it on to the back of your neck.

The family arrived at Fethiye early on Tuesday morning, just as planned, having passed the night in a modest pansiyon in Göcek. It was with pleasurable anticipation in their hearts that the couple drove along Suleyman Demirel Bulvari at ten miles an hour, with, in front of them in the middle of the road, an ancient tractor being driven doggedly by a stoical old man in a flat cap. It was with even greater pleasure that they beheld that city of white awnings which constituted the bazaar, erected overnight on either side of the canal, and somehow always the same.

The bazaar had, by a natural process of evolution, divided itself into the part that catered for the tourists and the part that catered for the locals, and it had grown extremely large. The part for the locals consisted mainly of some two hundred metres of stalls devoted to fruit and vegetables. Fat shiny aubergines were heaped up next to beans with pink pods, sweet peppers in all sorts of odd shapes and in every shade of green, okra, potatoes, spring onions, and succulent red tomatoes that actually tasted of tomatoes, and which were therefore quite unlike anything that you might find in a supermarket in Britain. Some tables specialised in olives, with a dozen different varieties heaped side by side on vast aluminium plates. There were stalls that sold white cheeses from capacious goatskins that still had the hair on them. You could buy honeycomb, chickpeas, pistachios, sun flower and melon seeds, almonds, henna, tea from the Black Sea, saffron, chicks and ducklings, tall brass spice-grinders, apple-tea, mountain tea and lemon cologne. Robert particularly loved the tool stalls, where you could buy elegant axe heads, hammers that double as chisels and nail-pullers, scythes and sickles, tack for horses and donkeys, folding clasp knives, cooking knives and heavy lengths of rusty chain. Both of them loved the tables laden with cookery implements, and could not resist the conical brass coffee pots or the double-decker teapots. In this part of the market the buyer was mainly left in peace, the prices were absurdly low, and one could drink sweet apple-tea amicably and with no obligation with the owner of each stall, until one's stomach was bloated and gurgling with it.

The tourist part did contain the stalls that sold bolts of cloth for the women to make their own skirts and headscarves, but otherwise it was an extraordinary bedlam. It had one very long straight section from either side of which branched many culs-de-sac of greater or lesser length. It was packed to the uttermost limit with tourists who artlessly believed that this was the authentic part of the bazaar, unaware that it was really a sort of commercial hellhole created specifically in order to take advantage of them.

The day was insufferably hot, and the conditions under the canvas alleyways were predictably appalling. It was quite airless, there were far too many people, and the harassment from the vendors would have been enough to drive even the Buddha to distraction. At the entrance was a loud fat woman who was selling gaudy, poor quality jewellery, and unpractised Europeans who had not yet learned the art of polite but adamant refusal were sucked in by her torrents of words as she forced them to try on earrings that they didn't want, until finally they could only escape by buying them. Susan palmed her off almost as if she were a rugby player, and the family forged ahead into that awful purgatory, whose one positive aspect might be that at least the overwhelming heat and jostle reduced Vinnie to abject submissiveness. His parents dragged him between them, and he came along miserably and sullenly, his eyes blinded by sweat.

A boy appeared in front of them, dancing about as he demonstrated a small brass toy that was something like a cross between a yo-yo and a spinning top. 'Very nice,' said Robert, pushing ahead. A man on the right suddenly and very loudly played the first inane bar of 'Happy Birthday to You' on a small toy reed instrument that sounded somewhat like a kazoo. A man on the left imitated birdsong on a whistle that was half filled with water. A very tall blonde Scandinavian girl walked past in a state of almost complete undress, a neat cut across the back of her shorts displaying a delectable white buttock. The local men stopped what they were doing and watched her pass with expressions of delighted amazement on their faces, their lust so absolute and ingenuous that it was almost respectful. All around, and at every stall, came Turkish voices trying out the only English they knew: 'Hallo, how are you? Look,

look, excuse please, very nice, very cheap. Engleesh? Where you from? Look, look, very nice, excuse, excuse, you look. Why you not look? Apple-tea? Here, I give you apple-tea, you look, OK? Too much good things! Looking is free!' A man selling nylon mats called out, 'Turkish carpets, you want Turkish carpets?' and Robert astonished him by saying in Turkish, 'Sorry, I don't have a house.' 'You speak Turkish?' demanded the man, addressing Robert's retreating back, as if speaking Turkish were against the local bylaws governing the conduct of foreigners. On her side of the aisle Susan fended off a persistent gentleman who purveyed counterfeit Chanel perfume, and Robert, on his side, fended off another who sold counterfeit Cartier watches.

'We've got to find Vinnie a complete set of clothes,' said Susan.

'Well, that won't be difficult,' replied Robert.

'I want to go home,' moaned Vinnie, completely over-whelmed by the suffocating atmosphere and the discomfiting press of people. His parents tightened their grip on his hands.

They found a stall manned by a jovial character dressed in a maroon cardboard fez and a gilded waistcoat covered in small mirrors that had been made in India. 'Better than Harrods!' he was bawling. 'Cheaper than Tesco! Lovely jubbly! All genuine fake! No problem! Nice and cheap! I give you change next year! Everything free … tomorrow!'

Laid out before him were passable imitations of all kinds of designer wear, with the logos of Lacoste, Reebok, Adidas or Nike shamelessly emblazoned across them. 'Ah,' said Robert, 'real Turkish clothes.'

Susan began to pick through the clothing, and the vendor descended on them like a vulture scenting a wonderfully ripe cadaver. He began to sift through the garments himself, thrusting items into Susan's face. 'Look, very good, very nice, very cheap!'

'It's all right,' said Susan, 'I am going to buy a lot of things anyway.'

The man in the fake fez endured a pang of disappointment over not having a chance to exercise his powers of pestiferation, but he soon left Susan and Robert in order to resume his wauling: 'Better than Harrods! Lovely jubbly!'

They bought four shirts, three pairs of trousers, seven sets of underwear, seven pairs of socks, and, from a neighbouring stall, three pairs of shoes, all at two-thirds the price originally demanded. From the stall next to that, and for the ridiculously low price of two million lira, they bought a cheerful plastic sports bag in the red and yellow colours of Galatasaray football club. Into this they put all the clothing they had bought, and then they struggled back through the crowd. Susan bought a pretty white headscarf, trimmed in blue, and then at last, back out in the sunlight, they found a refreshing breeze blowing in off the bay. 'Thank God we're out,' they said, both at once.

'My God, Robbie, your shirt is absolutely soaked!' exclaimed Susan, as he mopped at his brow with a handkerchief.

'It's like a bloody greenhouse in there,' said Robert, and Susan peered down her front.

'I've got sweat running down between my boobs,' she said. Vinnie spotted a blind man playing a tragic lament on the szass, and darted off in order to remove some of the hundred-thousand-lira notes that charitable passers-by had placed in his hat. Robert stopped him just in time, and, grasping his son's hand firmly, took him to the public lavatory on the green behind the

theatre, but at the foot of the mountain there are no cafés where you can buy Coca-Cola and chip butties. There is Incealiler instead, which has never emerged from the nineteenth century and has never wanted to. It has resolutely remained in the middle of nowhere, the authorities have continued to be more or less ignorant of it, and it is the sort of place where the women scuttle into their houses at the mere sight of an unfamiliar man, pulling their scarves across their faces as they go. Rare visitors find themselves confronted by the head-man, the Mukhtar, who, standing alone in the middle of the street like the sheriff in an old western, assesses the visitors and judges whether or not they are worthy of hospitality. He is a tall, dignified, semi-shaven, tattilyclad but redoubtable gentleman who exudes a kind of moral force and confidence that is completely extinct in the modern European.

Susan and Robert drew up in their car, leaving behind them a feather of beige dust that hung in the air along the track as far as the eye could see. The Mukhtar fully expected the foreigners to be the next worse thing to the devil, and was therefore thoroughly disarmed when Robert extended his hand and intoned, 'Salaam alekum.' The Mukhtar shook his hand and smiled, exposing dark brown, pointed stumps where once his teeth had been. 'Alekum salaam,' he said, adding the inevitable, 'Cay?'

No sooner had Robert settled in the cay-house than all the other men begin to appear, irresistibly motivated by that chronic nosiness which is so deeply engrained in the Turkish national character. They nodded their heads, saying 'salaam alekum' as they entered, and immediately set about discovering how many children their visitors had, where they lived, where else they had been, whether or not they liked Turkey, and how much their watches cost.

Robert and Susan had discovered the place on their first trip to that country, when they had been more adventurous, more easily seduced by the romance of vanished civilisations and melancholy ruin, and less concerned with the well-being of hire cars in general. Last time they had not drunk tea until they had been up the mountain and back down again, but back then there had been no Vinnie. On this occasion Susan brought him to the cay-house, but modestly and fittingly declined to join the men, drinking tea on her own, and hiding under her headscarf in the shade of a fig tree. The cay-house consisted of no more than a hard mud floor beneath an open-sided shelter whose roof was constituted of bamboo fronds cut from the banks of a nearby river, but it was none-theless the social focus for the community's men. A couple of them produced the inevitable backgammon board, and Robert attempted to make conversation with the Mukhtar, who was determined to maintain his position as principal host and poser of questions.

They made the usual exchanges, and then Robert reminded the Mukhtar that many years ago he had guided the young couple up the mountain in order to look at the ruins. The Mukhtar searched his memory, and smiled. 'Ah, yes,' he said, 'I remember you now. Your wife screamed when she saw a snake.' Robert was amazed at the man's accurate recollection, and immediately felt that an intimacy had been established between them. 'My wife is scared of snakes,' said Robert.

'Most women are,' replied the Mukhtar, 'and so are most men. It was the snake that removed us from paradise.' He nodded towards Vinnie, who was biting his own fingers and looking somewhat wide-eyed with uncertainty, and said, 'You have a very pretty child.'

Robert's Turkish was far from fluent, but he had picked up just about enough from tapes and from their frequent visits to Turkey. He had taken the precaution of working out in advance, with the aid of a dictionary and a textbook, exactly what it was that he had to say. His pronunciation would be ludicrous and his grammar eccentric, but he thought he would be able to make himself understood. He bided his time until the moment was correct.

The Mukhtar stuck his cigarette squarely in the front of his mouth and seized Vinnie under the armpits. He deposited the child on his knee and draped one arm over his shoulder, using his other hand to continue his smoking and tea-drinking. Vinnie sat there tamely, rolling his eyes and pulling faces, but otherwise well behaved, and Robert took a deep breath and summoned up his courage. 'Do you think you could look after him for a while?' he asked.

'Look after the child?' asked the Mukhtar, furrowing his brow.

'Yes.' Robert nodded. 'My wife and I have to go away and do ... something.'

'How long?'

Robert spread his hands in a devout gesture, and said, 'As God wills,' adding, 'A short time, inshallah.'

The Mukhtar looked at Robert unblinkingly, as if assessing the state of his soul, and then, without further question, and indeed without any word at all, he got up and crossed the stony street to his house. He lifted the latch, opened the door a fraction, and called out, 'Mehmet!' A smiling, ragged, barefoot, grubby, shiny-haired and bright-eyed little boy of about Vinnie's age appeared, and his father said a few words to him, motioning towards Vinnie with a loose wave of his arm. Mehmet came forward boldly and took Vinnie's hand. He had the same unquestionable air of command as his father, and Vinnie got up as if compelled. Hand in hand the boys disappeared up the slopes of the mountain, because Mehmet wanted Vinnie to see some especially big tortoises. Vinnie kept looking behind him, over his shoulder, but Mehmet gave him no choice, and in a few moments he was gone from view, disappearing behind the clumps of oleander.

The Mukhtar gazed after them and smiled. He had fond memories of running about on the mountain when he was a little boy, before adulthood, parenthood, authority and Islamic sobriety had imposed dignity upon him. 'Very good,' he said.

'Very good,' repeated Robert. He waited as long as he dared, and then drained the last few drops of his fourth cup of tea. He offered the Mukhtar a five-million-lira note, but it was waved away without consideration. He rose to his feet and shook hands with all present, repeating '*Allaha ismarladik*' to each one, and receiving the customary '*Gule gule*' in reply.

With a very odd feeling rising up in his heart he trod the stones back to the car, smiled reassuringly at Susan as she strapped herself in, and opened the back door. He took out the sports bag with the clothing in it, undid the zip, and got out his wallet. He removed one hundred million lira in five-million-lira notes, and put them in with the clothes. He deposited the bag on the ground, opened the front door of the car, hesitated, got in, and started the engine.

Two hundred metres up the road he stopped the car. He looked at his wife. 'Well?' he said.

She smiled wanly, but said nothing.

'This is the moment,' he declared. 'We have to decide now.'

'Do you think he'll be all right?' asked Susan.

'Turks always keep their promises,' said Robert, 'especially the rural ones.'

'I feel bad about deceiving them,' said Susan, biting her lip. 'How long did you say?'

'I said "a short time".' Robert looked straight ahead, and then he said, 'If you think about it, in the context of eternity, all times are short.'

This Jesuitical piece of sophistry convinced neither of them, but it made no difference. Susan began to cry, and he put his arm around her. 'You know what's really sad?' she asked finally. 'What's really sad is that I won't even miss him.'

'I won't either,' he said. There was a long silence between them, and then Robert said, 'We could always try for another one.'

Susan ignored the suggestion. 'It is the right thing, isn't it?' she asked. Her eyes implored him to say that it was.

'It's his best chance,' said Robert. 'In fact, it's probably his only chance. This is for him as well as for us.'

'The Turks are so wonderful with children, aren't they?' said Susan.

Robert put the car into gear and let out the clutch. In low gears they jolted, bumped and slid through the potholes and runnels until, half an hour later, they finally attained the main road.

As they turned left on to the tarmac and Robert accelerated through the gears, they experienced, quite viscerally, the blessed relief of lost time and lost life returning. Susan felt youth and well-being re-establish themselves in her heart like familiar friends. When they reached the mountains they would make a cheerful little bonfire of Vinnie's British clothes, but now they began to sing as they commenced the long but exhilarating journey to Izmir.

STUPID GRINGO

Jean-Louis Langevin strolled away from the Gold Museum, and reflected that Bogota was not quite as he had been led to expect. Someone in the office back home in Paris had said, 'They call it the city of eternal spring,' and so Jean-Louis had arrived in the expectation that cherry trees would be in blossom, daffodils would be nodding in the parks, and beautiful tropical girls would be out and about in states of partial undress. He sniffed the moist air, with its bouquet of carbon monoxide and gasoline, and was reminded that much of any spring actually consists of gentle and persistent drizzle. At any rate, this was apparently the main ingredient of the allegedly eternal spring of Santa Fé de Bogota. It had been raining in a desultory fashion for three days, ever since he had arrived, and the beautiful tropical girls were effectively concealed beneath woolly sweaters, raincoats and bright red umbrellas.

After three days he already felt like an old hand in South America, and laughed to recollect the wave of trepidation that had swept over him when his boss had come into the office one morning and announced that he was sending him to Bogota, with the idea that an office should be set up there, to market software packages all over the continent. Ideally, said the boss, such an office should be in a place like Rio de Janeiro, but the Brazilian currency had become exceptionally strong, making it too expensive to set up there, and Bogota was a fine cosmopolitan city with regular flights to every capital in Latin America.

'But I don't speak Spanish,' said Jean-Louis, hoping to be excused from this particular mission, 'and I'm sure the Colombians don't speak French.'

'They all speak English,' said the boss, scrutinising him in an intimidating manner, letting it be obvious that he had taken note of Jean-Louis' lack of enthusiasm. Jean-Louis began to blush. He certainly did not want to give the boss the impression that he was a laggard, or even a coward, but nonetheless some instinct of self-preservation made him say, 'My English is very poor, too, unfortunately. All I can say is "Where is the toilet?", "How do you do?" and "I love you".'

The boss laughed. 'The English only ever say "I love you" to their dogs. To each other they only say, "Shall we have tea?"' The boss clasped an imaginary Englishwoman in his arms and gave her a cartoon kiss. 'O chérie,' he exclaimed. 'Let's go to bed and have tea.' The boss turned to Jean-Louis and said, 'How the English have children, only the Good Lord knows.'

'It's virgin birth,' replied Jean-Louis. 'Perhaps it's more common as a miracle than one might suppose.'

'Anyway,' said the boss, 'they say that an Englishwoman can be tremendous as long as she's drunk. I was told this by a Greek. Englishmen are all homosexuals, of course.'

'Ah, Greeks,' repeated Jean-Louis, his mind drifting away to the terrible things he had heard about Colombia. What about that story that the police were exterminating the children who lived in the sewers? Jean-Louis seemed to remember that this had turned out to be a canard, a clever trick whereby an enterprising Colombian had screwed millions out of sentimental European charities. Well, what about all these political assassinations, and the kidnappings, and the violence of the cocaine mafia? He shuddered, and heard his boss saying, 'When you get there, you are authorised to hire an interpreter.'

Jean-Louis suffered terribly in the three weeks before he went to Bogota. Everybody seemed to know a Colombian horror story. 'I hope you've made a will,' they would say, or, 'I hope you're taking kung fu lessons,' or, 'I think that you ought to confess and take the last rites before you go. Just in case.'

Everyone had some helpful advice, too: don't walk in the backstreets even in daylight. If you hire a car, watch out for the people with guns who rob you whilst you're waiting at the traffic lights. If you travel out into the mountains, watch out for the bandits who hold you up at roadblocks. If someone approaches you in the street and talks to you, watch out for his accomplice who is behind you, picking your pockets. Don't go out wearing a watch, and don't take your wallet. Put your credit cards in your shirt pocket, and if you carry cash, roll it up and put it in your socks. Don't wear your wedding ring, but keep a couple of dollars on you so that muggers will be satisfied and leave you alone. If you don't give them anything, sometimes they stab you or shoot you out of pique, and they like dollars more than francs, pounds or pesos. And if you get stabbed or shot, you should refuse to have a blood transfusion because you might get Aids or hepatitis, so it's best to take a couple of litres of your own blood with you, and make sure that you also have your own hypodermic needles, because they tend to reuse old ones. And if you go to Barranquilla, watch out, because they've got the most virulent syphilis in the world. Oh, and another thing, 'I love you' is '*te quiero*', and they don't lisp on the 'c' sounds, as the Spanish do. So when you're in a bar you don't ask for a 'therve-tha' you ask for a 'cerveza', OK?

Beneath this barrage of information, much of it delivered with overt smirks of Schadenfreude, Jean-Louis began to feel like a condemned man, or like a workbench that has become dented from so many frequent blows of a hammer. He fell into a kind of agitated sadness, developed a valedictory attitude to the world, and allowed waves of nostalgia to wash over him. He remembered childhood holidays at the campsite at Luc-sur-Mer. He remembered a Belgian girlfriend who had accompanied him on an expedition to Saumur, and an Englishman whose friendship he had forfeited, idiotically, after a quarrel about whether or not Bonaparte would have lost the Battle of Waterloo to the British if the Prussians had not fortuitously turned up at a crucial moment.

Jean-Louis' wife noticed that he had become sad and wan, full of sighs and wistful glances, and so in the evenings she made him paupiettes de veau and alouettes sans têtes and pieds de mouton à la mode de Barcelonnette, in the knowledge that the blood draws up courage and optimism from the stomach.

Nothing could console him, however, on the evening of his last day in France. That afternoon he had heard scuffling and sniggering outside his office, and when he had gone out to investigate, he had found that his so-called friends and col-leagues had taped a spoof obituary and a funeral wreath to his door. When he had returned to his computer terminal and checked his email for the last time, it had been full of mock tributes, such as one hears at a burial. That night Jean-Louis made love to his wife with tragical intensity, and lay afterwards with his head on her stomach, romantically listening to the gurgling of her insides, and feeling very much like a little boy in need of a mother's consolation.

But now, here in Bogota, he looked back at all that nonsense, and smiled. It was true that Bogota was somewhat cold and wet, and not in the least bit tropical, but every Colombian he had encountered had been charming, helpful, amiable and rather shamingly cosmopolitan. Many of them spoke excellent French, in an accent that sounded strangely like Portuguese, and he had had several embarrassing conversations in which Bologna was compared to Seville, or in which Stockholm was compared to Venice. Jean-Louis had never been to most of the places in Europe about which Colombians seemed to be so enthusiastically knowledgeable, and on one occasion he had been forced to admit that he had not even seen the Pont Saint-Pierre in Toulouse, or the monument to the Girondins in Bordeaux, and had never got round to seeing the version of the *Mona Lisa* that was hanging in the Louvre. Colombians seemed to be very fond of poetry, too, and he had had to bluff his way through discussions about Baudelaire and Prévert.

Yes, the Colombians were charming. He had not had to eat in his hotel even once, and had received more invitations to people's homes than he could possible honour. The cuisine had surprised him; he had been told that he would be eating llamas and guinea pigs marinaded in spices that burned holes in the oesophagus, but actually the cuisine was wholesome and even a bit bland. Chicken with rice seemed to be the ubiquitous favourite, and it did not even contain any garlic. Fried slices of banana were much better than one had any right to expect, and yucca had turned out to be delicious.

Jean-Louis felt relaxed in Bogota. His stomach was contented, the weather was like Paris at the beginning of April, and the bandits at the traffic lights were either cleaning car windows, just as at home, or selling copies of *La Prensa*. Some of them appeared to be earning a living by selling the novels of Gabriel García Márquez, referred to familiarly as 'Gabo', so that at first Jean-Louis had thought people must be unaccountably preoccupied with the actress who just wanted to be alone.

It was true that his new Colombian friends kept warning him about the muggers – they had this strange gesture that meant 'Watch out for thieves', which consisted of pulling down one corner of the right eye with the forefinger – but it seemed to him that there was no sign of danger from anyone anywhere. The centre of the city was small enough to explore with the aid of a tourist map, and he had devoted happy hours to tourism that should have been spent exploring the possibilities for opening up an office for the marketing of software in Latin America.

Jean-Louis Langevin had been sensible, of course. He had put his credit cards in his shirt pocket, he had rolled up his cash and put it into his sock, where the notes chaffed him somewhat as he walked, he had left his watch and wedding ring in the hotel safe, and he had put a couple of US dollars in his trouser pocket so that any mugger could be sent away moderately gratified. Nonetheless, he was beginning to think that all these precautions were somewhat otiose, and that all the warnings and horror stories were simply the exaggerations of the inexperienced. He strolled away from the Gold Museum and back towards his hotel, admiring the sharp peaks of the mountains, and savouring the shafts of golden sunlight that were beginning to slice their way through the dirty grey clouds. 'Ah, at last, eternal spring,' thought Jean-Louis.

When he heard the footsteps behind him, though, approaching at a rate that was faster than a normal everyday walking pace, it was as if somebody had pressed a little button inside him. It was a button that switched off the sunlight, the mountains, the rainbow above the cathedral, the happiness of a casual tourist with time to waste. It was a button labelled 'fear', and suddenly all of Jean-Louis' senses went on the alert. Intently he heard the virile tapping of metal-tipped leather soles on the paving slabs. He smelled the scent of arepas frying in corn oil on the corner of the street. He tasted wet air in his mouth. His eyes rolled in an attempt to see behind himself without turning his head, and he felt a trickle of sweat abruptly course down the centre of his back and disappear into the waistband of his trousers.

'Hey, gringo,' called a voice behind him, and he flinched.

'Walk fast and don't turn round,' he told himself, 'act confidently, as if you know where you're going.'

'Hey, hey, gringo,' came the voice again, and he increased his pace. It might just be one of those importunate hopefuls who want you to help him find a job in Europe. He had had to cope with one or two of them already.

'Gringo,' called the voice again, this time with a clearly discernible note of irritation, 'gringo gringo gringo.'

Wasn't 'gringo' an insulting sobriquet for a Yank? 'If he just wants to insult me, then I won't stop,' thought Jean-Louis, who certainly bridled at the thought of being mistaken for an

American. The man was not saying it in an insulting fashion, however. It sounded vaguely friendly, perhaps even ironic.

Jean-Louis finally could not prevent himself from glancing behind, and he caught the eye of a large man in his early thirties. He glimpsed a yellow shirt with thin red pinstripes, grey trousers which were a little too tight about the thighs, and brightly polished leather shoes with ornamental buckles. 'Colombians,' he thought, his anxiety causing his mind to operate at hazard, 'always have nicely polished shoes.' The man was dark, like a Corsican, and seemed to be well muscled and fit. '*Merde merde merde,*' thought Jean-Louis, and he redoubled his pace.

'*Momentito, momentito,*' exclaimed his pursuer, '*espera. Mierda. Ay hombre, espera.*'

Jean-Louis' mind went blank, and he made no sense at all of these Castilian exclamations.

There are only two types of person in such an emergency, the fleers and the fighters. Jean-Louis spontaneously discovered that in his case the response was definitely flight. Reason skidded away like a car on ice, and he broke into a run. Some extraordinary inhibition prevented him from calling for help; he was actually embarrassed to yell '*au secours*' in a Spanish-speaking country, and how can you yell 'help' in English, when you are French, and French people naturally cannot pronounce an 'H' even when there is no crisis?

'*Hijo de puta loca,*' he heard behind him as the man also broke into a run, '*Cabrón. Gringóncho. Espera.*'

Jean-Louis ran, his feet blurring beneath him, and a copious cold sweat breaking out all over his head. He smelled his own rancid panic, and felt his eyes bulging painfully. Behind him he heard the steady and inexorable tapping of metal toecaps on stone, and the perspiration ran down into his eyes, blinding him. He wasn't sure, but it seemed to him that tears were coming from his eyes and mingling with the sweat. He wanted to pray, to call upon God or the Virgin, but all he could come up with, like a blasphemous litany, was, *'Salaud salaud salaud salaud.'*

Jean-Louis blundered on, cannoning off lamp-posts and astonished pedestrians, fending off stacks of cardboard boxes, overturning dustbins, whilst behind him the terrifying and implacable steel toecaps drew ever closer.

Jean-Louis felt a squeal emerging from his throat, like the sound of an injured pig, or a woman keening over a death, and realised quite suddenly that all his strength had gone. It was the altitude; no stranger can run for very long at three thousand metres, even when that stranger regularly plays tennis at home in Paris. He felt his legs turning to rubber, and his feet increase in weight until they seemed to be pulling his knees to the ground. Nausea overwhelmed him, and his heart leaped and thumped in his chest like a beast that has been confined and is bound on breaking the bars. 'I'm going to die,' thought Jean-Louis. 'O God, I don't want to die.'

Expending a last desperate overdraft of strength, he turned right up a side street, and ran straight into a dead end.

His hands spread out against the brick wall, Jean-Louis, blinded by tears and sweat, his lungs cramped and shredded, his legs shaking, decided officially that he was going to give up. He was not going to turn and run, and he was not going to turn and fight. He was going to turn around and allow himself to slide down the wall amongst the overflowing dustbins that suddenly seemed so inviting and enticing. To die and to sleep seemed to be much the same thing, and both seemed equally attractive. He was already sprawled amid the rubbish, weakly struggling to loosen his tie, when the man with the steel toecaps rounded the corner and stopped before him, panting a little, but not enough to prevent a radiant smile from creasing his face.

Jean-Louis looked up and saw an impressive row of white teeth, amid which there sparkled one that was made of gold. He saw sensual lips, dark brown eyes, an impressive and glossy black moustache, and a tawny skin that sprouted with thick and exuberant stubble. More thick hair sprouted from his chest where the top button of his yellow shirt was unfastened. He was not as big as Jean-Louis had first thought, but he had the stout and finely muscled forearms of a physically active man. Jean-Louis caught a fleeting impression of a chunky gold watch and several substantial gold rings.

The man reached down, and Jean-Louis whimpered and cowered, shielding his face with his arms. Mumbling in placatory desperation, he started to fumble hopelessly for the dollar bills in his trouser pocket, and thrust them towards the man with little nervous flicks of the wrist. '*Voilà, voilà,*' he gasped, and the man took them from him. He looked them over with mystified attention, shrugged, shook his head, and then leaned down and stuffed them perfunctorily into Jean-Louis' shirt pocket, where they joined his credit cards.

The man reached into his own trouser pocket, pulled something out, and waved it in front of Jean-Louis' face. The latter cringed, fearing that it must be a weapon, perhaps a knife or a derringer. Again he crossed his arms in front of his face to protect it, still blinded by sweat and terror, and heard the man sigh with exasperation: '*Hijo de puta. Su dinero. Eh, gringo.*'

In the midst of his fright, Jean-Louis became aware that
the man was actually tickling him. He was brushing something
lightly across the backs of his hands, and on the top of his head,
mussing his hair. Whatever it was that he was being tickled
with, it felt like crisp paper, and made a clean rustling noise like
sycamore leaves on a dry autumn day. As his wits reassembled
themselves, Jean-Louis began to realise that what the man was
tickling him with was a roll of banknotes.

He looked up uncomprehendingly, and then, astonishingly,
the man began to mime. He pointed down to his left foot, he
raised it, he flexed the elastic around the top of his sock, he put
the roll of banknotes into his sock, and then withdrew it again
and dropped it on the ground. He mimed spotting it and picking it up, and then he mimed running, waving the roll in front
of him.

All at once, understanding dawned upon Jean-Louis. His
hand went down to his sock, and he felt the now empty place
where his money had been concealed for safety. '*Mon argent?*' he
asked the man, and the man stuffed the money into Jean-Louis'
shirt pocket, along with the dollar bills and the credit cards.

'*Su dinero,*' explained the man again, gesturing towards the
wad where it lay in its new place of concealment.

New tears began to follow each other down Jean-Louis'
face. He would never know whether this was from relief or
gratitude or from bitter shame. The man reached into his own
pocket and produced a tooled leather wallet. Out of it he pulled
all his money, the scribbled reminder notes, business cards and
credit cards. These he returned to his own trouser pocket, and
then he reached into Jean-Louis' shirt and removed the latter's
cards, cash and token dollars. He tucked them into the empty

ROMANCE ON THE UNDERGROUND

Women are not like us; this is the first thing that you need to know. You should not be misled by having grown up with a mother and sisters, for they are not women in the sense in which I mean to speak. Mothers and sisters have no romantic interest in their brothers and sons, and so one's experience of dealing with them is quite useless when it comes to coping with the real thing. Now that you are fourteen years old, it is time for me to tell you that all through your life you will be perplexed by women, you will discover over and over again that even the most clear of your perceptions was not quite the truth, and you will undoubtedly go to the grave as confused and puzzled as you are at present.

Your mother tells me that recently you had your first real kiss, and that you found it slobbery and disgusting, like chewing a slug. I am not surprised; this is your first lesson, and one that you will probably never learn, which is that what you think you want from women is not what you actually want. Men want to go to bed with every eligible woman in the world, and when by a stroke of luck the opportunity arises, they often take it. But what happens? The experience might be disappointing, or even slightly repellent. This does not prevent us from sticking to the hunt, however, for at heart we are just dogs, and cannot help ourselves, even though we know both by experience and instinct that only some women are truly able to turn this animal act into something mystical and sublime.

Curiously, and perhaps fortunately, the woman who is able to do this for me is not the same woman who can do it for you, or for the man next door; the woman who is an enchanted being for one man may well be an entirely ordinary piece of work for another. Another lesson that every man learns, incidentally, is that these enchanted beings are not necessarily the most resoundingly beautiful. We all know this perfectly well from our own experience, but because we are dogs, and so easily deceived by our own eyes, we forget it over and over again, usually within a few seconds of relearning it. Time and again I have left a superb woman who was not quite pretty enough, only to be disappointed by a woman who was beautiful ... but I am sure that you do not wish to hear about what has happened to me.

On the other hand, now that I come to think of it, perhaps if I do tell you something from my own experience, it might help you to see what I mean about the rarer and more unusually beguiling kind of woman. The sad and tragic thing is, by the way, that somewhere along the line, sooner or later, one usually forgets what it was that made her so enravishing, and everything slowly becomes unravelled. But that's another matter.

I know that you are only fourteen; I don't see you as often as I would like, and I cannot put my hand on my heart and say that I know you as well as I should, but if you are anything like a normal fourteen-year-old, you probably think that the experience of someone who is inconceivably old, such as myself, is completely irrelevant. I felt the same whenever my father offered me advice.

Tant pis. That is the way the world is, and we cannot change it, but let us pretend that we are the same, not man and boy, but man and man, swapping tales about women, and then perhaps you will feel less like a youngster who is being lectured.

I have always loved women. If I pick up a telephone after a woman has used it, and her perfume comes back out of the mouthpiece when I speak, I am entranced by a delicious sensation of intimacy. When I go into the bathroom after a woman has been in there for two hours performing all those rites and mysteries of which I still know nothing, the atmosphere of feminine humidity arouses in me an inexplicable tremor of gratitude and affection. My imagination is full of women, even when I am supposedly working, and even during those few times when I have been trying to pray.

The world is bulging with desirable women, as you have no doubt noticed already, but there are some who have a special presence, as if the space they occupy has more intrinsic depth and reality than that of others. These ones are surreptitiously incandescent, they glow with an invisible light reminiscent of mountains, shortly after dawn, in a tropical land. When I encounter one of these, it is like being in a clearing in the Amazon when a jaguar strolls past, sniffing the air, or like going to the front of a boat, looking down into the water, and seeing dolphins curvetting across the bows.

There is a sense of rare privilege, an emotion that says, 'I am glad, after all, that I have lived.' Even though in some ways women have been the bane of my life, I still feel touched by grace whenever one of these exceptional creatures crosses my path, and it is about one such exceptional creature that I am going to tell you.

There is nothing picturesque about the railway line out from the capital to the airport. Part of the journey is underground, and all of it is somewhat slow and uncomfortable. Frequently one is hemmed in amid heaps of luggage, and usually there are crushes of foreign travellers whose voluble conversation creates a veritable Babel.

I was on this train one evening on my way to foreign parts, when my attention was caught by a young woman seated at forty-five degrees opposite. She had reclined her head against the glass partition next to the doors, and had an air of lassitude which intrigued me. I watched her. As you will have discovered already, we men cannot help watching pretty girls, it is as much a part of our nature as a horse's need to run, or a bird's to build a nest. The trick is to do it skilfully, so as not to cause offence; a woman likes to be noticed, but she does not like to be stared at as though by a predator. For the most part she enjoys practising the art of pretending not to have noticed that she has been noticed, and if, on the other hand, she is in a tetchy mood, she seizes equally the opportunity to practise a kind of disdainful indifference. The young woman of whom I speak noticed immediately that I was watching her, and gazed directly back into my eyes as though reading information from behind them. I was disconcerted by this frank counter-scrutiny, and was forced to look away.

Her own eyes were small, but very dark indeed, so that I could not see the pupils, and she had fine eyebrows that curved with classical simplicity. Her face was more pointed than it should have been in one who gave such an impression of natural beauty, for her lips were a little too thin, her nose a little too sharp. At the corners of her mouth she carried just the memories of a smile, giving her the air of one who is capable of sensual but harmless mischief. In the lobe of her right ear she wore two tiny studs, one a blue sapphire and the other a white diamond.

Her cheekbones were high and prominent, rending her face a hint of a Slavonic tilt, and her neck was very slender, so that I felt that I could have encircled it with one hand. Its delicate tracery of blue veins was just discernible beneath a very fine, pale and translucent skin. Her fingers were slim, with narrow nails, and in repose they gave the impression of precision and creativity; they belonged to hands that were those of a jeweller, perhaps, or a watercolourist. I imagined vividly that if I were touched lightly by them, I would receive a small shock of pleasure.

The girl's hair was indeterminately dark brown or ebony, very smooth and clean, and, parted at the centre, falling to the level of her neck. Her hair curled slightly inwards at the extremity, so that it seemed that it was caressing the skin of her neck.

My first impression was that she was quite tall. Certainly her legs were lightly made, with thin ankles, but with sleekly contoured calves and thighs that were set off to discreetly erotic effect by sensible black stockings. She was, in fact, dressed almost entirely in black, that being the colour of her cardigan and her short woollen skirt. Her shirt was white, however, and yielded not a hint as to the true conformation of her breasts. She wore two silver rings, and a necklace with a pendant that consisted of one large amber set in a silver heart.

Now, you can tell from the exactness of my description that I was captivated by her, and I watched her at every possible moment of the journey. Each time that we came to one of the many stops, I was once again surprised by my own relief that she had not alighted. I willed her to be there, coolly opposite me, right until I reached the airport.

From time to time she turned her head and regarded me with all the dignified and anthropological detachment of one who knows that she is worth observing in the train, and thinks little of it. When I smiled at her, she did not acknowledge it, but continued to gaze at me for a few seconds as though I were something that she had never seen before, but found only mildly interesting. I had a distinct suspicion that she was quite deliberately mystifying me. I had reason to think, however, that she was not as indifferent to me as she wished me to believe.

If you grow up to be anything like me, you will fall in love twenty times a day, but of course most of the lovely women in our lives are transient. We spot one in the market, or at the side of the road. Perhaps we are lucky enough to converse for a while at a social occasion. Even so, we are resigned to the ephemerality of these loves and desires, we are reconciled to taking gratefully what crumbs and morsels fate has afforded us, and we pass on, regretting what might have been, but with a regret that is sweet and poignant. We have not dirtied our illusions by diving into the turbid waters of a real flesh-and-blood encounter.

I was likewise stoically facing the fact that she and I would never become acquainted, and likewise I was experiencing those inevitable tiny pangs, when the train stopped at the airport station, and we stood up to leave.

I saw that in fact she was a very small woman, not in the least bit tall, for it had been only her slenderness that had created that impression. I saw also that she had an enormous suitcase, which clearly weighed a great deal. She struggled to heave it through the doors, and then managed to get a few yards before she dropped it, and looked about. I supposed that she was looking for a trolley or a porter.

I touched her on the shoulder and said, 'Please may I help? Your case seems to be very heavy.'

She looked up and said, 'Oh, it's you.' Her voice was light, with a trace of the countryside outside the city.

I shrugged and smiled, implicitly admitting culpability. I pointed to the case. 'Shall I take it?'

'What about your own luggage? Aren't you carrying anything?'

'I'm only taking this,' I said, indicating the small Gladstone bag in my right hand. 'I'm just going for the one night.'

She looked at my bag and said, with irony in her voice, 'I think you've mastered an art that I should study myself.'

She took my bag from me, in token exchange for hers, quid pro almost quo, so to speak, and we set off towards the moving staircase. 'What have you got in here,' I asked, 'books?'

'Yes,' she said.

'Makes a change from dead bodies,' I said. 'I'm bored with dead bodies.'

She laughed. 'There's no fun in dead bodies. Books are better.'

'Depends on the books. I can name quite a few that would make a corpse seem lively.'

She glanced at me sideways, and in a severe tone of voice that belied the easy tone of our conversation hitherto, she demanded, 'Don't you know that it's bad manners to stare?'

I was taken aback. 'It's only bad manners to be caught staring. I'm sorry, I thought I was being subtle about it.'

'It's a kind of oppression, when a man keeps staring at you. It's not nice.'

'What is it when a woman keeps staring at a man?' I asked. 'And I don't mean when you do that trick of looking straight at me as if I were an advertisement for soap in a vaguely familiar language.'

We were upstairs by now, heading towards the check-in counters, and we stopped in our tracks as if by mutual agreement. 'What do you mean?' she asked.

'I mean,' I said, 'that you were watching me the whole time, but you didn't think I'd noticed. So when you did your staring trick, you were just being a hypocrite, and you're being a hypocrite by asking me whether I don't know that it's rude to stare.'

'I wasn't watching you,' she protested, but a little feebly.

'You were next to the glass partition,' I reminded her, 'and you were examining me minutely the whole journey, by looking at my reflection in it. It's an old one, that. I've used it myself really quite often.'

She bit her lower lip, and cast her eyes to the ground. As an admission of guilt it could not have been more fetching. 'Damn it,' she said, 'you're observant.'

'You've been caught out,' I teased.

She spread her hands. '*Mea culpa.*' She looked up at me humorously, and caught me with those black eyes. We looked at each other in silence for some long moments, and then I spoke. I said things that under other circumstances I would not have dreamed of saying, and I looked away, and not at her, so that those things would be easier to express. Nonetheless, the situation almost rendered me somewhat incoherent. Normally I am a fluent talker, as you know, but she was so lovely, and time was so short, that I collected my words together only with great difficulty.

'I always look at women,' I confessed. 'I can't help it. If it's any excuse, I have reason to believe that all men are the same. Anyway, I look at a lot of women.' She smiled encouragingly, and I continued, 'But sometimes I see someone who is especially bewitching. I mean that she might have fathomless eyes, or lips that one could kiss for ever or she might have an air of being very adorable or very sad, or very wilful. You are one of those: a woman I would have to look at even if the penalty were death.'

'My God,' she said, 'he's telling me I'm a gorgon.'

'You're special,' I persisted, 'you're a wish-bringer.' I paused, but she seemed nonplussed, so I blundered on. 'Look, I'll probably never see you again, otherwise, believe me, I'm not normally like this. I mean, I wouldn't normally talk like this. What I mean is that, given the chance, I would be seriously infatuated. I'm sorry, have I said too much?'

She twisted her mouth and shook her head knowingly. 'Either you're a shameless flatterer or you're very sweet.'

'Men hate being called sweet,' I said, glad to shift the subject a little.

'Men are going to have to put up with it,' she replied.

'Have you got time for coffee,' I asked, 'before your flight?'

We drank our coffee in shared silence, as if subdued by what had been said, or as if cowed by the necessary brevity of our time together. She put down her cup and looked away across the tables, and sighed. She shook her head as if annoyed with herself, and delved into her handbag. She said, 'I'm going to do something my mother told me not to.'

I raised my eyebrows in enquiry.

'I'm going to give you my address. I'm going away for two weeks, and when I come back you can send me flowers. If I am impressed, I might give you a call. If you turn out to be a nuisance, though, I must warn you that I have two affectionate and solicitous brothers who are much bigger than you are.'

She handed me a card, and stood up. She leaned over, kissed me softly on the cheek, and walked away quickly without looking back.

When I returned from my trip I decided to go and have a look at her address; one can learn much about someone from the outside of their house. In this case I was to be frustrated, since she had plainly only just moved in. The 'For Sale' notice was still there, lying on its side on the tiny scrap of front lawn. It was a pleasant but ordinary house in a pleasant but ordinary suburb, and I guessed that she had bought it with the probable intention of having a lodger or two to help her out financially.

I stood there in the drive, noticing how tatty everything was, and how desperately untended the garden seemed, when I remembered what she had said about the flowers. I was fortunate indeed that it was early summer.

Suffice it to say that when she came back she found hanging baskets full of lobelia and pelargonium. She found the grass mown, and she found the beds weeded and planted out in the cottage style, with delphiniums, aconitum, periwinkle, aubrietia and Rose of Sharon. When she telephoned me, the first thing she said was, 'Lucky I hate gardening.'

Now, I have completely forgotten why I was telling you this story. I think it was something to do with women in general. No? Oh yes, you are right, it was to do with the world's most exceptionally Circean women, and how a woman who is an ordinary piece of work for one man is a goddess or a princess for another. I should think, for example, that you would never have imagined, if I had not told you this story, that that is what your mother was to me.

MAMACITA'S TREASURE

The old midwife swung her legs over the side of the bed and rubbed her eyes with the heels of her palms. A cruel and implacable light had already invaded the house, stamping a brilliant rectangle upon the floor where the door stood open. She moved her feet a little to one side, so that the sun would not scald them, and took an experimental breath of air. She breathed out with resignation, reconciled in advance to one of those days when each inhalation would be a desiccation of the lungs, so that little oxygen would be absorbed. One would have only to move a hand to brush a wisp of hair from the eyes, and the sweat would pour down one's back and between the crease of the buttocks, it would trickle down from the neck between one's breasts, and one would thank the Good Saviour for the gift of eyebrows that prevented the salty water from running down from the forehead and stinging the eyes.

They called her 'Mamacita' or 'Abuela', 'Little Mother' and 'Grandmother' being the only terms that seemed adequate to express the respect and affection in which she was held. Her true name had long since been forgotten, sometimes even by herself, and she possessed the happiness of one who has been useful all her life even though none of her youthful aspirations had been fulfilled. She had never had a husband, had never had money, had never learned to read, and had never travelled further than the town of Domiciano, but on the other hand she had delivered three generations' worth of babies, had never starved, and had never made an enemy.

Mamacita sat on the edge of her bed and looked down at the speckled and loosened skin of her hands. She held them up to the ruthless light and marvelled at the way they had become transparent. One could almost see the bones and blood vessels. She tried to still the tremor that had been worsening for the last ten years, and thought back to the time when they had been strong and self-confident, easing infants from the womb as if they possessed a knowledge that she herself had never consciously acquired. There was barely a soul within a day's walk that had come into this world without her firm hands cradling its head, and that included a fair number of the animals. It was true that for the most part it was only the women who bore the curse of agonising birth, but it did happen from time to time that a foal tried to come out the wrong way, and that was when Mamacita might be called.

Mamacita had never been accused of sorcery or malice, even upon those few occasions when the child or the mother had died, and she was quite famous for some spectacular feats of life-saving, the most celebrated being the occasion when Don Balcazar had insisted that the child's life be saved rather than the mother's, so desperate was he for an heir. Mamacita had stood up to him, pronouncing that the child would be a mooncalf, and a curse to him for the rest of his life, and she had ordered his brothers to take him away so that she could save the life of his wife, who lay upon the bed delirious and begging for death.

Mamacita sent everyone out of the room, and cut the infant to pieces inside the womb, taking the limbs out one by one, until she had assembled upon a towel the complete body of a devil with a horny head and a monkey's tail. So horrified and repentant was Don Balcazar that he had crossed the sea to make a pilgrimage to the shrine at Santiago de Compostela, and after his return he had produced a family of six normal children. From Spain he had brought back a silver crucifix to present to Mamacita, and she had hung it above her bed, the only rich thing that she was ever to possess, and which now hangs in the side-chapel of the Church of Our Lady of Sorrows at Domiciano, with a yellowed and curled morsel of paper stuck on to the wall beside it, explaining its provenance and the story of the mooncalf.

On this day Mamacita reflected wryly that in the dry seasons one longs for rain, and in the rainy seasons one thirsts for the brutal sun. Still, the advantage of so much dust was that one could draw in it, and she hoisted herself slowly to her feet so that she could go to the table. She bent down to check against the light that there was indeed enough dust, and made a pair of experimental lines just to make sure. Then, pursing her lips, she drew the details of the map that she had remembered upon awakening. On the other end of the table she set down a plate, a small cup and a steel tumbler.

Struggling with the matches and the knobs, she lit two rings of her petrol cooker, and on one she toasted a tortilla that was half wheat flour and half maize flour, whilst on the other she set a diminutive saucepan in which shavings of panela and grounds of coffee would boil up to produce a redolent brew that would wake a dead horse. She reached into her cupboard and drew out a half-bottle of aniseed-flavoured aguardiente, which she poured into the steel tumbler. She knocked it back in one slug, experiencing all over again, as she had every day of her adult life, the delicious and startling assault of strong alcohol on an empty stomach. This was a morning ritual in every household, and was designed to kill intestinal parasites. Those that were not killed would be stunned and horrified, and such small revenges had their own satisfaction.

Mamacita sliced a *platano* and fried the pieces in corn oil. She wrapped them in the warm tortilla, and masticated slowly and painfully with her toothless gums. There was something comforting about eating the same breakfast every morning, she reflected, and besides, when she went to see Don Agostin, he would undoubtedly give her some avocados to take away with her, and she would have the glorious obligation imposed upon her of eating all of them before they turned black and slushy. Her mouth watered at the thought.

Mamacita sipped the sweet strong coffee. It was like tasting the distilled essence of one's entire country: the tyrannical rain, the arrogant earth, the perverse savannahs, the obstinate jungles, the supercilious mountains, the playful rivers. She lit a cigar, and felt the sweet fumes fill up all the empty spaces in her skull.

Her breakfast finished, she ventured out into the white light, her puro still clenched between her teeth, and squinted for a moment. She shuffled slowly past the chickens that pecked and squabbled in the dust, and entered the little shop where Conchita sold alcohol and machetes. Both women raised a hand in greeting and drawled, '*Buen dia.*'

'I want a pencil and a piece of paper,' said Mamacita. 'I want a good pencil, and the paper should also be good.'

'I will give you a piece of paper,' said Conchita, 'but such a pencil will cost from two to ten pesos, depending upon how much of it is left. I have a good one here' – she produced a pencil from a drawer – 'and with careful sharpening it will last a long time. Who knows? Perhaps a year. The cost is four pesos.'

Mamacita inspected the pencil suspiciously. It was important to appear knowledgeable even if one was not. She turned it over in her fingers and said, 'I will give you an avocado from Don Agostin's finca. I don't have it yet, but I will have it later.'

Conchita sighed. She had tried for years to consolidate a habit of cash-for-goods amongst her customers, but the village had only been well connected to the outside world for a few years, and the old habits had not been easy to change. Still, an avocado was not such a bad idea, so she said, 'OK, an avocado, but a big one.'

'A very big one,' agreed Mamacita, chewing the end of her puro, 'but don't forget to give me the paper.'

Conchita reached under her table for a spiral-bound notebook of the type used in schools, and carefully tore out one sheet, which she handed to the old midwife, who took it reverentially between thumb and forefinger. 'Paper,' she said, in the same tone of voice as one says 'thunder' when it is about to rain.

Back in her little dwelling, Mamacita carefully transcribed on to the paper the map that she had drawn on to the dust of the table. It was very difficult. If one pressed hard, the fingers went into a clench that was hard to control, but on the other hand, if one pressed lightly, then the lines were faint and wobbly and did not go in the right direction, and neither did they stop at the right place. '*Hijo'e puta,*' she swore to herself, revelling in the delightful luxury of using in solitude an obscenity which never in her life had passed her lips in public.

Mamacita scrutinised her completed work with some dissatisfaction, and felt the bitterness of ill-education mingle with the bitter taste of tobacco on her tongue. Her eyes were not in any case as good as they had been, and, when she peered hard, the lines faded and duplicated themselves, wandering about like ants and slipping away like snakes. 'It will have to do,' she told herself, 'and Don Agostin can always improve it if he wishes, with God's help.'

She put her chart into her mochila, and hung it from one shoulder. It was made of heavy white linen by the Indians in the foothills, and had a pretty double-stripe around its top, in natural shades of maroon and green. She went out once more into the white light, and made her way towards the beginning of the long track that led down to Don Agostin's hacienda. On one side was the reedy swamp where small caimans lazed and grunted, only their snouts and their arched eye sockets above the level of the water, and on the other side was the field with the fallen trees where one of Don Agostin's mares was cavorting about with her foal. Mamacita laid her mochila on the grass, muttered a charm against coral snakes, and sat down on it, forgetting that this would crumple the map. She was waiting for Don Agostin's tractor driver, who passed this way several times a day, toing-and-froing between the different halves of the farm.

Mamacita arrived at Don Agostin's feeling like a queen. The tractor was a venerable but lovingly tended bright red Massey Ferguson, a very large one, and today it had had the bucket mounted on the front so that it could be used for earth-moving.

Mamacita had been installed in the bucket, and then raised high in the air, so that she became lady of all she surveyed. It was perilous, no doubt, and once or twice she had experienced tricky moments involving low-hanging branches, but it had been marvellous to be able to see the world at speed from such a novel angle, and she had also contrived to pick some lemons, a large grapefruit and two avocados. It was not stealing, she reasoned, because Don Agostin would not have minded. Besides, the cooling effect of the air as it passed her by made her feel just a little irresponsible on such an otherwise oppressive day.

It was difficult to maintain dignity as Mamacita was lowered to the ground in a series of jerks, but she clung grimly to the side of the bucket and continued to puff at her cigar with every affectation of nonchalance. The vaqueros who were saddling up their ponies and mules at the tack-house gave her an ironic cheer as she stepped to the earth, and she beamed at them shyly but brightly, so that for one evanescent moment they caught a glimpse of Mamacita as she had been when young, when her father had become accustomed every night to having to chase away the boys who came to sing rancheros outside her window.

Mamacita crossed the flagstones shaded by bougainvillea and tapped on the frame of the door. Through the fine green mesh that let in the air without also admitting the insects, and which served the place of glass in that tropical inferno, she could see Don Agostin himself, hunched over his papers at the dining table. Beyond him she could glimpse the cook in the kitchen, apparently skinning an iguana.

At the sound of her knock, Don Agostin called 'Enter' without even looking up, which struck Mamacita as a little

Mamacita came straight to the point. 'I have come to sell you a dream,' she said.

'A dream,' repeated Don Agostin.

'Yes,' she said, 'I have dreamed something, and you are the only person I can think of who can take advantage of it, since you have a Land Rover.'

Don Agostin was curious. He had been to a fine school in Cali and could have been a café intellectual anywhere in the world were it not for his duty to the family farm – he could cite instances from philosophy, and quote Neruda with the best of them – but he had learned to listen with more than half an ear to these dogged campesinos. He had become familiar with their syncretistic religion, their fantastical beliefs and quirky rituals, and could not in all honesty deny that sometimes they knew things in a manner that could not in the ordinary run of things be called knowledge. Had he not witnessed his own cattle cured of an inexplicable epilepsy by an itinerant mountebank who kissed them on the mouth and muttered secrets in their ears? It seemed that in different parts of the world there were entirely different laws of nature. You could not apply scientific principles in this place, any more than you could cure a European cow by kissing it.

'What is the nature of this dream?' he enquired. 'Naturally one must inspect the goods before purchase.'

'I dreamed of gold,' she said. 'I know exactly where it is.'

'Don't you want it for yourself, Abuela? Why don't you go and find it?'

Mamacita gestured loosely towards the foothills. 'It's over there. I think that one would need a Land Rover, or even mules. It's too far for me, I'm an old woman, and I don't have the means. That's why I thought I would sell the dream to you.'

'Is it a huaca, by any chance?' asked Don Agostin, referring to the huge urns in which the Indians used to bury their dead.

'I can't say,' said Mamacita, 'all I know is that I saw the exact spot, with a golden light above it. Like an angel.'

'It's funny,' mused the patron, 'but I have always thought of angelic light as being more silver than gold. One has such funny ideas.'

'There might be silver,' said the old woman. She rummaged in her mochila and produced the rumpled piece of paper. 'I drew a map, and I am prepared to sell it to you.'

'And how much are you asking?'

'I am asking two thousand pesos, and a share of the find.' She looked at him resolutely, the cigar, now extinguished, still protruding soggily from the corner of her mouth.

The patron whistled. 'Two thousand? That's enough to pay a vaquero for ten weeks. And what share do you want?'

Mamacita raised all ten fingers, and then folded back seven of them. 'I want three out of ten, because three is the number of the trinity, and lucky. Also, three is made by the adding of the first two numbers, and therefore it is a very perfect number.'

Don Agostin was pricked by curiosity, and also by a feeling of obligation. How many times had his mother insisted that he would not have survived his birth if Mamacita had not greased her arm with lard and reached in and turned him? Two thousand pesos was not too much money to help such an old lady for a time, and indeed, perhaps he should settle one hundred pesos a week upon her in any case. The good that one does in this world lives beyond the grave. 'I will give you three thousand pesos, and a fourth of the share,' he said, willing himself not to regret it the moment that it was said.

'It is too much,' said the ancient midwife, her mouth working, and her rheumy eyes flicking from side to side.

'I insist,' he said.

'Who am I to contradict the patron?' she asked rhetorically.
'I accept, but not willingly.'

'Your reluctance shows great graciousness,' he said.

'I want it notified,' she remarked suddenly. 'I want it done
before a magistrate.'

'I am a magistrate,' said Don Agustin, mildly offended
that she appeared not to take his word. In fact, Mamacita had
recently become impressed by this business of bits of paper, and
it appealed to her to have an official one.

'Forgive me, I forgot, Don patron, but I would like a piece
of paper all the same.'

Don Agostin removed a notepad from beneath his heap of
paperwork and wrote in a beautiful cursive script: 'I, Don Agostin Leonaldo Jesus de Santayana, certify that on this day I have
purchased from … .' Here he stopped and said, 'Forgive me in
my turn, but what is your real name? I cannot write "Mamacita"
on an official document.'

'It's Liliana,' she said, 'Liliana Morales. But Mamacita is
better.'

The patron continued to write ' … Liliana Morales, spin-
ster and midwife of this village, the right to a map indicating
a place of treasure, revealed in a dream, for the sum of three
thousand pesos and a fourth of the gross sale value of the aforementioned treasure, should it be found. Witnessed by God and
by the aforementioned Liliana Morales.' He dated it, signed it
with an exuberant elaboration of curlicues, and passed it over
to her, saying, 'Keep this in a place where you can powder it

with insecticide, or the termites will eat it, and we will have no agreement. Now, perhaps you would permit me to see the map?'

Mamacita passed it over, and Don Agostin scrutinised it. He felt both amused and cheated, for it was no more than a web of errant scribbles. 'I think you should explain this,' he said.

Mamacita leaned over and jabbed at the paper with a trembling forefinger. 'This is a stream,' she said, 'and this is a goat track, and that is a rock that looks like a man, and this is a bush that is dead and has been burned, and this is a black rock that looks like a jaguar, and here you will find the skeleton of a horse, and this is where the sun rises, and at this place between all these things, you will find the treasure.'

The patron noted all of this, naming the features on the map. 'Perhaps you could give me an indication of distances,' he said.

Mamacita ran her forefinger over the scribbles, reciting, 'This is ten paces, this is five minutes' walk for a grown man, this is the same as from here to the waterfall, and this is about the length of a lemon tree's shadow an hour before sunset.'

'That seems very clear,' said Don Agostin with an irony that he knew she would not perceive. He scratched his head with the pencil.

Mamacita rose and offered him her hand, which he kissed again, this time less gallantly than before, as he was beginning to suspect that he had somehow been nudged into making a fool of himself. Mamacita reminded him, 'Don't forget the four thousand pesos.'

'It was three thousand pesos,' he said, 'and a fourth of the treasure.'

'O, forgive me, it's my old brain. It's not what it was.'

'An understandable error,' he said drily. He left the room and returned a few minutes later with a sheaf of five-hundred-peso notes, which he handed to the old lady. She had never had so much money in her life, and she counted it shamelessly before rolling it up and stuffing it carefully into the bottom of her mochila. 'Another thing,' she said, 'whilst I am here. I have heard that you have a good crop of avocados.'

'Of course,' said the patron, 'you shall have some.' He called through to the cook, 'Emma, bring through some avocados, would you? Nice big ones with no blemishes.'

Mamacita was returned to the village by the same means that she had arrived and went promptly to pay Conchita for the pencil. Conchita took the avocado and prodded its apex appreciatively. 'Just a few hours and it will be perfect. Thank you, Abuela.'

'I can sell you back the pencil now,' said Mamacita. 'I don't think I'll need it again, and if I do, I can always come back and buy it again. I will sell it back to you for three pesos and another bit of paper, and then you can sell the pencil again for four pesos.'

'You old fox,' exclaimed Conchita admiringly.

What came of all this? Don Agostin and his foreman made several exasperating expeditions into the foothills, greatly perplexed to find hundreds of rocks that might look like a jaguar or a man. Stupefied and baffled by the heat, disorientated by insects, startled by armadillos, lacerated by thorns, they blundered from one incandescent rock to another, futilely stabbing with a pick at the unyielding baked pale earth of each location that seemed propitious.

They found numerous goat tracks, many a stream, a fair quota of burned bushes and a large number of horse skeletons, besides the skeletons of cattle, donkeys, mules, pumas and the gruesome mummified cadaver of a ginger-haired human being clad entirely in the leather garments of an old-fashioned hunter. In view of this evidential prodigality, Don Agostin felt just as incapable of blaming Mamacita for misleading him as he felt of ever finding the treasure. He eventually developed the intention of trying a few more times, but somehow never quite got round to it.

As for the old midwife, she had little immediate use for such a large sum of money, and she sealed it into a small clay pot, which she buried in her backyard at a depth of two hand-spans. On her spare piece of paper she indicated its whereabouts by means of another wobbly and indecipherable map, which she placed in the same termite-proofed drawer as her contract with Don Agostin, before going to sell the pencil back to Conchita for the agreed three pesos.

After Mamacita's death, her nephews found the contract, and wondered what she might have done with the money, but they could make neither head nor tail of the scrap of paper covered with shaky lines and arcane blobs, so one of them who had been caught short used it in the outhouse and then dropped it into the cesspit.

One morning, not long after the funeral, Conchita awoke, having dreamed that there was buried treasure in the place where Mamacita used to live, and she took a lift on the tractor down to the hacienda, to try to sell the notion to an obdurately sceptical Don Agostin.

OUR LADY OF BEAUTY

The sepulchre was situated in the communal graveyard of Santa Madre de Jesus in the province of Santander. This graveyard was, on account of its location upon the side of the volcano, almost unique in that everybody was buried upright and above ground, enclosed by four slabs glued poorly together by a pinkish mortar ground from tufa and mixed with lime and water. Often this mortar would crack, and crumble away, so that by the light of a match or a taper the local children could peer into the darkness of the tombs and wonder at what they saw. Inside, draped with spiders' webs and often with snakes coiled around them, they would behold the mummified ancestors of the village; they would discern wisps of gossamer-like hair sprouting thinly from yellow scalps so shrunken that through the rents one could see white bone. There were shrivelled lips drawn back in the parody of smiles and snarls, and one could wobble the teeth in their sockets by poking at them with a stick.

Sometimes one could see a cloth around the jaw, knotted at the top of the head to prevent the mouth from falling open, and some of the corpses had coins in the eyes for the payment of the boatman who ferries souls across the last waters. Occasionally, for a reason unknown, the corpse's head would have turned so that when one peeped through the chinks one's heart would leap to the throat with the horror of discovering that the cadaver was staring back as though it had been waiting there for years for a glimpse of the light in living eyes. There was one child in the pueblo who, having seen this, was pursued relentlessly by nightmares until one night she ran shrieking from her father's house and was lost in the maw of a jaguar. Her grave is out on the edge of the cemetery, and is so small that one can lift off the lid and see the pathetic pile of scored bones held together with the leather thongs of ligament and cartilage. Sometimes her father lifts it off himself to place orchids and blossoms of bougainvillea within, and he raises the skull in his hands and talks to it, kissing the lips and tenderly arranging what is left of the long dark hair. In this way he overcomes the tragedy of separation and accustoms himself to death.

We are a village accustomed to death. Every generation has borne witness to a new devastation. In my grandfather's time there was the plague of cholera that swept away all of his relatives, and the village was so cruelly emptied that he had to marry somebody from another place. In my father's time there was the violence; one band of political guerrillas after another came through, raping, robbing and murdering, starting and continuing vendettas that flare up all over again to this very day. In my village no one votes in elections any more because of the memory of what outrages ensue from political idealism; when the communists tried to start a foco here we gave them away to the army, and then we got rid of the army by telling them that there were more communists towards San Isidro. We don't want any politics any more, and, if we voted, it would be a vote to be left alone.

In my own time we had the whooping cough that carried away one half of the children here and left so many empty cradles and broken hearts, and there was the avalanche when the south escarpment of the volcano broke away and flattened the end of the village where the brothel was. They say it was a judgement of God upon a house of infamy, but it carried away a good many fine men and women in addition to the revellers, not all of whom were very bad in any case. I might add that many of the whores survived, and that one of the dead was the priest, who had gone there to preach against the immoralities. It is because of the illogicality of God that around here we still worship the orishas, whom we can at least understand.

Above all, it is our cemetery that accustoms us to death. We grow up with our dead still visible amongst us, and one of them in particular. His name is Don Salvador, and he came here as a missionary about one hundred and fifty years ago. He lived here for forty years amongst us and had many fine children by various women; they say he was still a fine seducer even in his seventies, and when he died we made him a saint. It was not only out of gratitude that he had saved us from the damnation of the hell of the heathens, but also because he taught us so many things. He instructed us in writing and reading, he taught us Spanish, he taught us how to build bridges supported upon columns, and he taught us the art of making love. Before he came it was forbidden to make love in any position except with the man on top, but he instructed the local women in the use of the tongue and in the possibilities for different positions. He taught that if God had proscribed these positions He would have constructed our bodies in such a way that they would have been impossible to perform, and very soon the old ways were abandoned. It is because of him that I am called Salvador.

The principal reason why we made him a saint was that he was so fertile. We remember not only his many children and his bull's appetite for love, but we have been told by our grandparents that wherever he passed the flowers burst into bloom, the crops burgeoned, the trees grew heavy with fruit, and women and animals grew heavy with the unborn.

So when he died they never sealed up his tomb, but only placed the slab in front of it, in a groove that was chiselled out of the rock. The path to his resting place is worn smooth by those who have crawled to it on hands and knees to beg for children. One would slide the stone away and kiss his feet and his hands, begging his intercession with Our Lady of Conception. A garland of flowers would be always upon his head, and, despite the temptation to steal parts of him as holy relics, I have to say that nobody ever did, and he is still intact to this day. As a man there are things to which ordinarily I would not admit, but such is my devotion to Don Salvador that I state that it was he who cured me of my impotence with my wife, and I know many others for whom he has done the same, whose names I will not tell you in case it brings them shame.

In addition to Don Salvador's continued presence amongst us in his tomb, we carry him upon a litter around our fields twice a year when we do our planting. We sing hymns and songs, and we throw jugs of water on the ground, and it must be said that despite all the disasters we have suffered in the past, our crops, our animals and our women have never failed us, except for the time when the new priest forbade us to perform the ceremony, saying that it was a pagan sacrilege. Nowadays nobody pays any attention to the new priest, and not just because of this.

Don Jose always contradicted the teaching of Don Salvador. He has even told us that Don Salvador must have been an impostor and an Antichrist. Don Jose wants us to be ashamed of our bodies and to go back to the practice of making love furtively in only one position, he wants us to stop using herbs to avoid unwanted pregnancies, and he wants to frighten us with stories about infernos of fire when we are dead. But we remember the teachings of Don Salvador which have been passed down to us, and we argue with Don Jose, saying that we have been told about God being a God of Love. When we pass Don Jose in the street we say, 'Be joyful in the Lord,' and his face just grows more sorrowful. We do not like to see a man so lonely, but that is the price of his perversity.

It happened one evening that there was an earthquake. It was not a serious one, even though it seemed terrifying at the time. There was a distant rumble like thunder, and everything started to shake and sway. In my hut the tin mug slid off the shelf and fell on to my wife, and the bell in the porch of the church began to ring on its own. Some of the animals panicked, and there was a bull that escaped from his corral and ended up entangled in the creepers at the edge of the forest. Everybody ran into the street, and most of us could not keep our balance, so we all fell over. Old Aldonaldo remained in his hammock smoking a puro and laughing at us, and he seemed to be the only stationary object in a world that had become as restless as the sea. He was calling out, 'Ay, ay, ay,' and enjoying every minute of it.

As it was the dry season, a great cloud of dust was shaken up, and we all got covered from head to toe in white dust. We were all coughing and falling about when Don Jose ran out of his house crying out, 'Repent, repent, the Kingdom of God is at hand. Woe to the inhabiters of the earth and of the sea, for the devil is come down unto you, having great wrath, because he knoweth that he hath but a short time.' No one was more disappointed than Don Jose to discover afterwards that there had been no damage to speak of.

In fact, the only damage was to the cemetery, where the slabs in the front of the tombs had in most cases fallen away. In some of them the bodies had fallen out forwards and were splayed upon the ground like withered drunkards or like the casualties of a battle, but in most of them the dead were still upright.

We wandered about the cemetery awestruck. The corpses seemed to be leaning casually against the sides of their habitations, and despite their mummification, their yellowness, the transparency of their skin and the whiteness of their bones, they seemed extraordinarily full of life, all except the recent corpses, which reeked horribly and dripped with a foul slime whose colour and odour comes back to me in bad dreams. We put the slabs back on those ones first, partly because of the offence to relatives, partly because of the stink, and partly because the vultures were showing an interest. Afterwards they perched forlornly on top of the graves, reminding me of how I felt when I could not crack a Brazil nut as a child.

Seeing the corpses brought the village back to its history. There were people there that had been all but forgotten, but now the living were wandering amongst them, recognising shreds of clothing, characteristic missing teeth, seeing the machete cuts of old murders, the broken bones of accidents. We were saying,

'Ay, that is Alfonso who lived by the river, who got bitten by the mad dog and who was in love with Rosalita,' and, 'Ay, ay, there is Mahoma, who arrived from nowhere with his strange religion and took four wives, and there is the holy book written in squiggles that he carried about with him and that he read from the back to the front,' and, 'Look, this is Saba who was so beautiful that two men killed themselves out of love for her, and then she took up with Rafael who had only one arm.' It made many old folk happy to see their old friends again.

But one man was more strangely affected. In the oldest part of the cemetery a grave had opened, the identity of whose occupant nobody could fathom, and who was a miracle. She had her eyes closed and she was very beautiful. People nowadays when they tell this story always say that she was in a perfect state and that she was as fresh as the day before she died. They will tell you that her lips were as moist as if she had just eaten a mango, and that she smelled of flowers and of vanilla, but that is not exactly how I remember it. I recall that her lips were dry, as they are when one wakes on a hot morning, and that she smelled of a house that has been shut up and never cleaned for years. People will tell you that her limbs were supple and full, whereas I recall them having the stiffness of an old lady. Otherwise, what they will tell you is mostly true.

I suppose it is possible that two centuries of death might have turned a dark woman white, but it seemed to us that she was a white lady because her skin was white like the flesh of a cassava, she had restrained lips, and her hair, although it was black, was very long and straight. Also she was tall, so she could not have been an Indian woman. She was clothed in a kind of textile that we had never seen before; it was very finely woven, and although it was now a yellow colour and crumbled to the touch, it had obviously been very rich. About her waist she wore a red sash, and on her feet were black slippers embroidered in gold wire.

We accepted her mysterious presence and her lunar beauty as a miracle, but without too much excitement, since this is, as everyone knows, a land where anything is possible and everything has happened at one time or another. We made her a saint, like Don Salvador, and we made a groove at the front of her tomb so that the door could be slid aside, with the idea that our women could pray to her for their beauty and for that of their daughters, that it might last for ever. We called her Nuestra Señora de la Hermosura, and it seemed reasonable to include her in our history as the favourite wife of Don Salvador.

But my brother Manolito was never the same man again. I was with him when he first saw her, and I remember vividly how strange his reaction was. He was a dark man, but he turned pale. He caught his breath, and he told me later that truly his heart ceased to beat for a second or two, so greatly did it leap in his chest. He looked at me with a wild expression, and then made a kind of expansive gesture, as though he were showing me into a richly appointed apartment. '*Fijate,*' he said, inviting me to look, as though I had not already seen.

'She is very beautiful,' I said, but he looked at me again as though I were stupid.

'She is exquisite,' he replied; it was the first time I had ever heard him use a word as poetic as '*exquisita*', and I laughed at him.

'Don't fall in love with a corpse,' I said, 'she will be very boring in bed.'

Manolito seemed to take the comment seriously. He put his hands together, as in an attitude of prayer, and said, 'She is lovely beyond the dreams of flesh. One could love her in the spirit and be satisfied.'

'You are loco,' I replied.

From that day forward Manolito used to go and visit her every evening and sit with the women who were praying to her for everlasting beauty. Like them he kissed her feet and arranged flowers in her hair, and he would linger on after they had gone, until I would have to come and fetch him away to eat his supper. I would find him sitting before her in the sunset, the red gold of the sky lending the glow of life to the woman's face, and often I would sit awhile and fall with him under the enchantment of that celestial face.

I will describe to you shortly the impression made by that face, but firstly I must tell you why she was so special to Manolito.

I cannot remember a time when he had not held in his mind the image of the lady he always referred to as 'my woman'. It must have started when he was about twelve years old. We shared a bed in those days, and we would lie there before going to sleep, listening to the crickets and the owls, and the coughing of the jaguar, and often he would talk about 'my woman', describing her to me. He told me how she walked with him after he was asleep, holding his hand, teasing him, play-fighting with him in the fields, kissing him on the cheek before he woke up or went on to another dream. For him, 'my woman' took on a reality so powerful that he never took a great interest in any other, not even in Raimunda, who could not get him to marry her even though she went to bed with him and got pregnant on purpose. Naturally I laughed at him and called him a dreamer, but he was sincere in his belief, and one day he told me that he had made love with 'my woman' for the first time, and that it had been the most beautiful experience imaginable. 'I promised to love her faithfully for ever,' he told me. 'From now on there will be no one else.' Naturally, I said that I had heard nothing and seen nothing during the night, and he showed me a bite on his arm that he claimed she had put there in sport. I said, 'You bit yourself, brother,' and he went to great lengths to prove to me that the imprint in his arm was beyond the reach of his mouth, and anyway the imprint was different from that made by his own teeth. In the end I gave in, just to keep him quiet.

But on subsequent nights I was awoken by him heaving and gasping beside me, moaning endearments, quivering with passion, and generally doing all those things on his own that my parents always did together when they thought that we were not around. It was at that time that I took to slinging a hammock outside under the silk-cotton tree, just to get a night's rest, and it was from that time that people began to notice his perpetual expression of sublime contentment and refer to him as 'the angel'. As for myself, I doubted his sanity, but I was his brother, and so I accepted him as he was, as a brother should, and I even envied him his nights of ecstasy, since I had never had any such myself, even with a phantom.

Manolito only had to see the corpse once to know that he had not waited and loved in vain. The materiality of 'my woman' seemed to him to vindicate what he had always known but had never been able to prove even to himself.

But you should not get the wrong idea and start thinking that he transferred his sexual attentions to a dead body, because

that is not what happened at all. He visited the body because
it had once been the habitation of 'my woman'; he visited it
because it made solid the stuff of dreams, as though the dream
in itself was too ephemeral, too filmy, too evanescent to take
hold of when he was not dreaming it. And at night his passion
increased until the whole neighbourhood was awakened by the
cries of his blissful consummations, and people began to protest
to my parents about the ferocious animal noises, so that my
brother had to move out and build himself a hut on the edge of
the cemetery.

Perhaps you will understand my brother's obsession when
I tell you that it was indeed a very perfect corpse. The eyes were
closed, but Manolito knew that the eyes were violet. There was
a perfection of symmetry in those features. The long black hair,
parted in the middle, flowed down either side of her cheeks,
reminding me of the way a stream flows when seen from a high
mountain, in the gentle curves of nature. The fact that her eyes
were closed accentuated her appearance of preternatural peace and
tranquillity, of the utmost repose, as though she were alive
and in contemplation of something supremely happy. Her eyebrows had obviously never been plucked in vanity, and yet they
arched like rainbows that spring from the nothingness of the
empty sky. At the upper tip they tapered so finely that one could
not say precisely where they finished, and at the bridge of the
nose they were full and dark, reminding me of the silky fur of a
fine black cat.

Her nose was straight, with the skin stretched so finely
upon it that it had the quality that one perceives when looking
through the body of a candle held up against a bright light. Her
cheeks were a little shrunken in death, which served to lend an

to calm its irascibility. It seemed that it was a god who had no longer any appetite for sacrifice or for activity, and even when it finally came back to life it did so with such gentleness that none of us felt terror or fell upon our knees to plead with the illogical Christian God or with the orishas. Of course, Don Jose was rushing about in a frenzy. He was shouting, 'Behold, I am against thee, O destroying mountain, saith the Lord, which destroyest all the earth; and I will stretch out my hand upon thee, and roll thee down from the rocks, and will make thee a burned mountain. And they shall not take of thee a stone for a corner, nor a stone for foundations, but thou shalt be desolate for ever …' Don Jose was very pleased that the cemetery was being consumed, because he disapproved of the intercession of Don Salvador and Nuestra Señora de la Hermosura. In fact, he once wrote in paint on Our Lady's tomb, 'Mystery, Babylon the Great, the Mother of Harlots and Abominations of the Earth.' Don Jose disapproved of female beauty, and he knew all the most depressing bits of the Bible by heart. But the rest of us just stood and watched from a safe distance, without any sense of mortal danger, until suddenly I remembered Manolito. The lava was flowing not down towards the village, but towards the cemetery.

I confess that I did not run and arrive half dead with breathlessness and apprehension. I strolled over, knowing that Manolito had more sense than to lie in his hammock with molten rock lapping at the doorposts. I went just to check that he had made good his escape, and found him watching the spectacle safely to one side and fanning his face with his sombrero. 'Ay, brother,' he said. 'It is all going to one side, and our dead are safe. It is quite something, is it not?'

Unfortunately at that moment there was a kind of belching and gulping noise, and a new fissure opened in the rocks above the cemetery. With consternation in our faces we watched the magma squeeze like dung out of its imprisonment, curving and solidifying, hissing and steaming, and we both had the same thought.

'I will rescue Don Salvador,' I said, 'and you must rescue Nuestra Señora.' I ran to the tomb and slid the stone away in a desperate burst of strength, and I carried the saint away in my arms with time to spare even to go back and fetch one of the hands that had dropped off and the lower half of the left leg as well. I was very pleased and was congratulating myself when I saw that Manolito was still struggling with the slab of the tomb of his beloved. I was about to rush and help him when I saw that I could never make it there before I was consumed in the advancing furnace of golden flame. All I could do was shout above the rumbling of the entrails of the earth, and watch my brother perish.

Manolito did not run. The slab gave way at last, and I saw him size up his chances at the last second. He did what I would have done under the circumstances: he stepped inside the tomb and drew the slab after him, hoping that the lava would pass him by and that he would be protected by the stone sepulchre. If he cried out, I could not hear it above the groans and cracks of the rocks.

I have often thought about the poetic manner of his death. He died in the arms of the woman he had always loved, attempting to save her. He died before age had diminished him, and he died in a fire as incandescent and overwhelming as his own passion. If he had cried out in that inferno I would like to imagine that it would have been the same kind of cry that he used to make at night in the embrace of his woman.

We made him a saint, we have many songs about him now, and around here we refer to a lover as a 'manolito' or a 'manolita', much as in Costa Rica they refer to youngsters as 'romanticos'. I go often to show the young people the place where my brother and his beloved embrace so deep beneath the rock, and I never fail to say that if they want to know the way that her hair fell down about her face, they have only to look at the beautiful curves that the lava made as it flowed and set above the cemetery where our ancestors slept.

THE COMPLETE CONTINENT

I never knew precisely why Mama let herself get inveigled into it, but I have my suspicions. I suspect that it was because my mother was so pious when she was young, and she took Father Alfonsin's *pronunciamentos* to be the very voice of God Himself. Father Alfonsin was a dried-up old bird of a man who knew of life only through what he heard in the confessional, and it was widely believed that he held strong views about contraception and about the absolute duty of all women to spread their legs at their husbands' whim. About the practicalities of this and the pitfalls he cared nothing, and I remember the scandal about poor Teresa Montera. The doctor told her that if she had another child it would kill her, and she went to Father Alfonsin to ask dispensation to use contraception. This latter told her that she had an absolute obligation to increase the number of God's faithful on earth, and that God would care for her in childbirth. He quoted that bit from the Bible about Onan spilling his seed on the ground, which everyone knows is irrelevant, and he made her feel such a sinner for asking about it that she came away thinking that she was dirt and weeping into her serape. Even her husband was angry, and swore that he would rather pay for it in hell than see his Teresa dying in parturition. The couple introduced a moratorium, except on those days when fertility was improbable, but that still did not stop her from becoming pregnant for the fifth time.

There is a joke amongst Father Alfonsin's flock, which is: 'What do you call someone who practises the Catholic rhythm method of contraception?' And the answer is: 'A parent.' Well, it came true for Teresa and she refused to abort it when she found out that she was expecting. Needless to say, she died as predicted, and the baby died as well, so that the number of God's faithful on earth was not increased one jot; in fact, since the child was dead before it had time to be baptised (and went straight to limbo, one presumes) the number of the faithful was actually diminished by one. The husband Rafael took a potshot at Father Alfonsin with a hunting rifle, shouting that he had murdered Teresa, but he missed and someone took the gun away from him until he calmed down. In the end Rafael took up with some protestant evangelicals and joined them in railing against the Pope every Saturday in the plaza. When he got sick of them he gave up religion completely and joined the National Secular League so that he could stick their flysheets up on the walls of Father Alfonsin's house after dark. They even had it guarded all night by a little group of vigilantes, but they never caught him doing it even though everyone knew that it was him.

My father was an extreme patriot. He not only passionately praised and adored his own country, but he felt the same way about all the other countries in Latin America. When they had wars and border disputes he would cry and wring his hands as though it were a rift within his own family, and during the Malvinas War he supported Argentina even though he knew next to nothing about the rights and wrongs of it.

Everyone else was saying 'Who cares? Those Argentines are all crazy bastards', but my father actually sent money to Galtieri to support the war effort. We could not afford it, and I have no doubt that the money ended up in some general's private bank account in Switzerland or in Rio de Janeiro.

It just happened that when my older sister was born there was a craze for naming one's children after a country, and so it seemed only natural that she should end up being called Colombia Carmelita. She was the one who grew up with the morbid terror of butterflies. She was black-haired and very pretty, with a laugh that would have shaken our windows if it were not for the fact that we only had shutters. We brothers used to torment her by catching morpho butterflies and dangling them under her nose, and she used to run about with her hands over her face, shrieking and crashing into the furniture. I feel sorry about all that now, but it seemed very amusing at the time. Papa took her to the doctor about it once, but he came up with some stupid theory that the cause was anal repression or something, and Papa told the doctor that he needed a psychiatrist for saying such an idiotic thing. In any case Colombia was hardly anally repressed, if my memory serves me well about all the tricks that she used to get up to.

Mama was only fourteen when she married Papa, and she went along with all this childbirth business because she thought that was what it was all about, until circumstances forced her to develop a mind of her own and start thinking for herself. When I arrived it seemed amusing to both of them to call me Peru so that I would match nicely with Colombia being called Colombia. Colombia says that when I arrived she was very jealous, and asked Mama to throw me away. When Mama said that you

cannot do that to babies, she asked her to put me back. Eventually Colombia got used to me and treated me like an animated
doll. She used to carry me around and take my nappies off so
that her little friends could pull my penis and watch me peeing,
but she stopped doing that to me when Argentina came along
and snatched her attention. Argentina was the one who ran
away with the gringo and went to live in California.

It seemed logical to fill in the space between Peru and
Colombia by calling the next child 'Ecuador', especially as he
was a boy. Ecuador looked like my grandfather, and he eventually confounded everybody by becoming a spiritual healer,
though he never could heal anybody in his own family. I went
along to one of his sessions once, and found the experience
very disconcerting. He was mumbling away in a language that
sounded like the gobblings of a turkey, and blowing smoke over
people's bodies. In the end he got into a fight with one of his
patients' husbands, and lost an eye. After that he gave it up as
too risky a profession, and he took to touring the country with
a suitcase, selling mechanical toys for a company in the capital.

The next one was named Bolivia, but she died of diphtheria
before anyone could save her, and consequently the next girl
who was born was called Bolivia Segunda. She was the boring
one who sat around all day doing nothing, but she was quite
pretty, and so she married a rich farmer and just carried on sitting around doing nothing. He thought that she was the ideal
wife, because she could not even be bothered to argue.

With five children, or six if you count Bolivia, a change
began to come over my mother. It was obvious that she had had
a surfeit of childbirth, and her spirit grew restless. She was only
twenty-two years old, and yet she had bags under her eyes,

her belly was distorted and flaccid, and her breasts were evidently drooping from so much suckling.

The first symptom of her change was a prolonged lapsing into silence. I remember that she spoke hardly at all for months on end, she rarely went out, and when she served meals she would thump the dishes down in front of us so that the food slopped over the table. My father would remonstrate with her, but she would glare at him defiantly, eat her own meal without enjoyment and then go and sit on the porch with a book. She mostly read romances and the Bible, but then she discovered Mario Vargas Llosa, and I suppose his books served to open up the world for her. She began to have political and social opinions, and argued with my father's point of view even in front of guests. He would say, as if by way of excuse, 'I have an intellectual wife.' He used to say that quite proudly, but when the guests were gone he would become patronising and tell her that her inexperience and her youth made her naive. She would scowl in disgust, and there would be yet more lengthy silences.

After Chile took two years to arrive, my father began to suspect that my mother was barricading her womb with contraceptives, and he called in Father Alfonsin to deliver her a lecture. They were under the big ceiba tree, sitting at the table, and I crept up behind the tree to overhear them. I did not understand much of what was said, being so young, but I remember the priest raising his voice querulously and coming up with all that 'These-matters-are-in-the-hands-of-God' stuff, and my mother was disputing with him and crying at the same time, saying things like, 'I am being treated like a brood animal, I have no life of my own.' Father Alfonsin was also lecturing my father, telling him of his husbandly duty to moderate his bodily passions for the good of his soul, but the general drift of his opinion was that if it was God's will that my mother should suffer so many children, then that was what she must reconcile herself to.

There followed a period when it seems to me in retrospect that every child was the product of rape. We children used to huddle together in our two beds, listening in terror as my mother shrieked and my father overturned the furniture. There were terrible thuds and crashes, and in the morning my mother's face would be covered in bruises and that of my father in scratches. They would remain grimly polite to each other, but during moments when she thought that she was alone my mother would weep into her skirts. More and more frequently my father would arrive home very late, crazy with drink and an unaccountable bitterness, and the fights would resume once more. The children of this period were Paraguay, Uruguay, Brazil and Venezuela, and I believe to this day that the only reason that mother did not leave was that she loved us desperately despite all the suffering that we brought and the ravages that bearing us wrought upon her body.

It was then that Gerard entered into the life of the family. He was an engineer who came from France, and he was a very talented man in many ways. He arrived at exactly the time as the economic crisis was beginning to bring the country to its knees. I seem to remember that the only conversation one ever overheard was about 'the economic crisis'; this crisis has never ended, and even though I was so young at the time I heard so much about it that I eventually grew to understand what it was all about, and I even understood in the end what 'two thousand per cent inflation' meant. From my father's point of view it meant that there was no chance of ever getting spare parts for the farm machinery, as the peso lost all its value against foreign currencies.

Gerard was one of those remarkable men without whom poor countries could not operate at all. This was because he knew how to reclaim machinery that was utterly defunct. He knew which parts of one engine could be adapted to fit an engine of a completely different make, he knew how to add things to oil and gasoline so that engines ran more smoothly, and it was even said that he could bore a cylinder by hand with perfect precision. Anyway, my father first got to know him when his tractor cracked a piston and packed up, and Gerard replaced the piston with one that he got from an old Yanqui lorry that had been rusting in the river for years. It was a masterpiece of improvisation, and my father brought him home to eat and take a few copas. I think that he paid him with chickens, since pesos were worth nothing.

Gerard was very handsome and cultivated, and he charmed the whole family right from the start. My mother was fascinated by him because of his Gallic manners and his ability to make her feel that her intellect was respected. It turned out that he too was crazy about the novels of Mario Vargas Llosa, and in addition he was able to talk about all sorts of intellectual movements in Europe in a very interesting manner. I do not mean to imply that here in our country we occupy a cultural backwater, because that is not true. Gerard himself used to say that we knew by heart more poetry than the inhabitants of any other nation. It was just that Gerard never took simple opinions as his own; he was always full of the complexities of apparently simple issues, and my mother found this a refreshing change from my own father's straightforward opinions. My father too enjoyed his conversations, and we children adored him because he would bring us gifts of pieces of old engines, all polished up, to use as toys and ornaments. I still have a piston from a Russian motorcycle that I use as an ashtray, which he gave to me on my saint's day.

Gerard had black hair, a pencil moustache, and glittering brown eyes. He suffered terribly from the bites of our mosquitoes in the rainy season, and Mama used to fuss over the sores, worrying that they would ulcerate. He became a frequent guest at our table, and I believe that to some extent he enlightened my father as to my mother's worth. He used to lean over and ask my mother's opinion of things, treating her answers with perfect seriousness, and often admitting that she was in the right. My father began to do the same, and we all noticed that Mama seemed happier.

It was Gerard who brought up in conversation the fact that all the children were named after countries, and he joked, 'Are you intending to give birth to a complete continent?'

This was the first time that anyone had had the temerity to hint at what was publicly considered to be the truth of my father's mania for children. Everyone saw for themselves that he did not lavish much paternal love upon us, that he ignored us for the most part, and allowed my mother to do all the work. When Gerard asked this question, my father said, 'Yes, a complete continent,' and my mother said, 'I will have no more children.'

There was an embarrassed silence at the table, and then Gerard made light of it, and said to my mother, 'There would be only three more countries to go.'

My mother replied, 'But Guyana was British, Guiana was French, and Surinam is Dutch. I think that the Latin countries of South America are quite enough. There will be no more children.'

My father was a little drunk at the time, and he treated my mother's remarks as a joke. He said, 'What about Panama and Costa Rica and Nicaragua? What about El Salvador and Honduras and Guatemala? And Mexico? What about them? It would be fine to have them too. And what about the Malvinas?'

My mother threw her eyes to the heavens, and Gerard said, 'Take pity upon your poor wife, Pablo, and upon your children.'

My father was annoyed. 'What about our children?' he said. 'They are happy enough. Do not interfere in our family affairs. And what of my wife? She is fed, and she does no more than a wife expects to have to do.'

He glared at Gerard, but Gerard did not back down. He stood up and put his hands on the table; he raised an eyebrow and replied, 'Ten children in two beds is not civilised, Pablo, and neither is wrecking one's wife's health with childbearing and overwork.' He left the table without finishing his meal, and my father did not speak to him again until the tractor broke a main bearing, and forced him to. But that did not stop Gerard from turning up when my father was away, and talking to Mama in the kitchen.

Papa forced Mama to have Guyana and Guiana. I am sure of that because there was so much shrieking and crashing about during those two years. Mama was always bruised and tearful, and when she called in the doctor to try to talk to Papa and work out whether he was suffering from a mania, Papa went completely loco and broke all my mother's possessions.

He threw the doctor out for impertinence, and from that time the doctor refused to help us even when little Venezuela seemed to be dying of a fever.

Mama was pregnant again when Papa was killed. No one knows exactly how it happened, but his body was found with a gash from a machete halfway through his neck. His assailant had taken his wedding ring and his money-belt, and so we all assumed that it was a robbery, although this did not stop the gossip when people noticed that Mama did not weep at the funeral. I remember seeing his glassy-cyed body laid out on the table, and not being able to feel anything at all. Colombia Carmelita told me in private that she was glad he was dead, and I did not know what to say.

There was a peculiar gaiety about Mama's period of mourning. She wore black and a solemn expression, but her mouth curled up at the corners with the hint of a smile, and she seemed happier with this pregnancy than she had been with the last ones. She would lie in her hammock in the evenings patting the hump protectively, laughing her tinkly laugh, and allowing Gerard to bring her tisanes and massage her feet. They smiled a lot, and stopped exchanging confidences whenever one of us children appeared. Bolivia Segunda started to call him 'Papa'.

When the baby appeared in the world everyone automatically referred to her as Surinam, even my mother, but things had changed. She was doing more of the farm work herself, and she left Surinam to Colombia Carmelita to look after for most of the time. But she loved the baby passionately, and she would dandle it on her knees and coo at it, calling it all sorts of pet names that seemed almost too sentimental. She also spent a lot of time seeming to be putting things in order, such as tidying the house, counting the sheets, selling off the surplus cattle, and so on.

Then Gerard disappeared and was not seen for a month, and then Mama disappeared too, with Surinam. She left a letter which said:

My dear children,

I leave all that I have to you, and I trust in Colombia Carmelita to be a mother to the family, as I trust in Peru to be a father to it. Both of you are old enough to inherit your patrimony. I will send you an address to write to when I have finished travelling, and I beg you not to miss me. One day you will understand that it is not only babies who have a right to be born.

I want you to know that I have remarried, even though the period of mourning is not over, and I have decided that the new baby's name is not Surinam.

With all my love, Mama

PS The baby's name is 'Francia', and it is my last.

TWO DOLPHINS

La Caboca Amadea was a connoisseur of earth; to each one of us the gods apportion talents according to caprice, and those of the gods with little intelligence (but impressively whimsical innovative genius) apportion talents of great interest but of even greater uselessness. When Exu decreed that Caboca Amadea should become a gourmandiser of soil, he did it with so little thought that he did not even remember to remind himself to keep an eye upon the consequences of his humorous gift, and so he was as surprised as everyone else when he discovered what had transpired.

From the time when Amadea was a very little black-eyed girl with tawny skin and hair perpetually wet from diving for turtles in the inundated forest, she was developing not only an infallible sense of direction amongst the tangles of trees, but was also learning to tell by taste her exact location. Beneath the water she could take a handful of the earth that was forest floor for only five months of the year, and surface with it. Shaking the water from her hair, she would first sniff the soil, appreciating its organic odours, its degree of fetidness, its proportion of sand, its perfume of submarine worms and the excrement of fishes. Then she would begin to devour it, slowly at first so that its warm tastes could mingle upon her palate, and then greedily so that she could feel it parading musically down her cormorantine gullet. This filled her with such delight that afterwards she would imitate the shriek of the hyacinth macaw, because nothing else could summarise her bliss.

Amadea learned in this way the exact taste of every barra within the range of her people, and because of this she became desired by every man, for with her in the canoe it was impossible to become lost, and one could go fishing far and wide, since even when one was beyond the limits of the known world, Amadea could tell from the savour of alluvial silt and the direction of the current the precise location of home.

At first people disapproved of her intemperate consumption of soil, because it was a sacrilege so to consume the body of a god. But Nenu declared after much thought that the Earthmother was not consumed, but transformed into a rich and valuable manure by passing through Amadea's gut. When the cabocos accepted this opinion of such an old and indisputably wise woman, Amadea accepted it happily as well, and thought of herself as the handmaiden of the Earthmother as well as the High Navigatrix of the sodden forest.

So it was that her pride grew mightily, and she heaped with contumely the humble offerings and inducements of her forlorn suitors, who prized her even more greatly the more she scorned and insulted them. She would send them away with the haughtiness of a young queen, and the judgement that she would never marry until one day a man appeared who would give to her a soil so exquisite that she could not resist him.

This is why for so many months so many young men of that tribe were seen wandering so far from the known parameters of their territory. This is why three fishermen were lost to caimans, one disappeared in the rapids, and one other died of despondency amongst the orchids and lianas, to be consumed in sections by a tigre that stayed by the corpse for days in order to see off any rivals for the dusky meat. This is the reason that Amadea became a connoisseur of soils from places where she had never been, from places as far away as Rondonia and Nuestra Señora de la Selva; but none of these soils, however aromatic, however doctored with infallible aphrodisiacs and irresistible love-potions hard-bargained for with cascabeles and brujos and wise women ever satisfied her regal longing for the most exquisite earth of the world, which would win her heart and cause her to grant the lifelong benediction of her nakedness.

Until one evening when she grew weary of the fiesta where Nenu was in the great hut drinking ayahuasca and vine-bark in order to determine the instructions of the gods, in order to become possessed by the spirits of ancestors from whom people were requiring advice as to the whereabouts of their lost knives and the biggest fish, and in order to travel the earth outside of her body and bring back news of the great events of the world that it was better to avoid.

Amadea went to the sandbar and wept. So great was her loneliness amid all that chanting and dancing, all that divination and sortilege, all that music from the men's hut, for so great was her longing for the man who would release her from her impossible vow. 'I am,' she cried, staring through her tears at the space between the stars called 'the Tapir', 'fourteen years old, and already within me I am stirring for a child, for a man's love, for a man's loins, for the hot spurt of childseed, for a lover's embrace in the forest and in the smoke of the hut. I am alone

peaches. She ate the soil slowly because she was drawing out
the pleasure of the savour of mangos, of three-toed sloth, of
comelon, of venison in a sauce of juniper berries and Greek
yoghurt.

She smiled up in the moonlight at the *bufeo*, who said
nothing as yet because in normal circumstances he spoke
in squeaks and whistles, and did not want to alarm her with
strange speech. His hand was still outheld, but now because it
was an invitation to her to take it, which she did, pulling him
down upon the sandbar and caressing his skin so finely muscled
from so much swimming.

Amadea made love with the dolphin every night upon the
sandbar, and became accustomed to his silence and the feel of
his slender embraces that stirred her so profoundly that during
the day she grew tumescent beneath her uluri just in thinking
about him and envisioning the events of the evening. When
the rains ceased and the waters receded into the courses of the
rivers she followed him and lived her caboco life on the shores
of unknown parts, swimming with him by day and cavorting
with him amongst so many other fish, until once more the rains
came and the waters rose up and flooded the forest, carrying
them back to her own stilted village.

The *bufeo*'s child grew strong in the village, but Amadea
was not there to care for her. The child Venu was raised amongst
the cabocos whilst her mother lived carelessly, immersed in the
waters and immersed in the *bufeo*'s silent love. Venu spent all
her life astonished by what she saw, because she was half *bufeo*,
and *bufeos* have very poor eyesight. With her human eyes Venu
experienced the world as a perpetually astounding panorama
of colours, because half her mind was *bufeo*, and, because half

her mind was *bufeo*, she would sit by the sandbar of her conception, listening with wonderment to the world of the singing fish beneath the waters, feeling the same longing as Amadea her mother had done so many years before. She felt the same longing even after the missionary men with the black clothes, the stern faces and the pathological hatred of life and its joys, took her away and gave her to nuns who attempted fruitlessly to prevent her frequent escapes to the river, and eventually cast her out at the age of sixteen because of it, which was how she found herself working as a secretary to an oil company, where she had enough leisure to sit for some of the day in a tropical reverie, listening to all the high-frequency squeaks that no one else could hear, and mesmerised by the fact that everything had a colour.

*

In the same year that Aurelio saved the life of the sub-chief Dianari by hacking at the sucuri snake that was attempting to suffocate him by constriction, in the same year that Aurelio was therefore adopted by the paje and taught all the secrets of Navante sorcery, in the same year that Amadea conceived Venu upon the sandbar, Anane the paje conceived Rebu by a female dolphin.

Anane was not a feared man because although he was a paje he understood that compassion was the secret of peace. He knew that upon occasion it is better not to be compassionate, which was why he never disapproved of the killing of white explorers who brought lethal diseases, and which was why he was as proud as anyone else that his people were tolerant enough to learn as much as they could from explorers before they were killed.

Anane was so compassionate that he had once lain absolutely still for a fortnight to allow a nest of mice to hatch in his hair, and he had once taken the unprecedented step of declining to rape the wife of a man who had raped his own wife. When he saw the suffering upon the woman's face, he had chosen instead the right to strike the rapist who was not permitted to resist. And instead of striking the man across the head with his bordana, and killing him, he had struck him across the chest and only broken a few ribs.

It was Anane who had taken yague and consulted with the tribal ancestor, Mavutsinin, to confirm that the village should be laid out in a crescent and that the moon was made of oropendola feathers. It was Anane who had agreed that from now on a knife should be called a 'couteau' to honour the memory of a French explorer who had arrived half-eaten by lechmaniosis leprosy, but who had touched their hearts by knowing how to pat their chests in greeting, which made him an honorary Navante so that he was allowed to die in peace whilst Anane blew smoke over his body and chanted so that his ancestors could come all the way from France to collect his spirit, thus preventing him from becoming a disorientated ghost lost for ever amongst the creepers and the heliconius butterflies.

On the day that Anane conceived Rebu by the female dolphin, he had risen from his hammock in the communal choza at precisely the correct time, which is to say that it was precisely the time that he actually felt like getting up. He had been awakened because some people had already got up and opened the opening, so that now there was not enough smoke for a man to sleep in peace. He left his wife sleeping in her hammock beneath his own, and their child sleeping in the hammock below that with his ocelot curled up on top of him for warmth and company, and went out into the crescent of huts. He straightened his necklace of jaguar claws and his anklet of bark, and went straight down to the river to take his first bath of the day, where he noticed that the female dolphin was rolling lazily in the water.

When he came out he squatted down whilst Aurelio the displaced Aymara Indian who was his apprentice picked out all of his ticks and lice, as was his obligation as a social inferior. Then, with the feeling that this was to be a day of celebration, he plucked out every body hair he could find and mixed up pigments with which to decorate his body. He mixed piquia oil and annatto, and painted himself red and yellow; he mixed wood ash and put in the white bits; he took genipapo, and drew in the blue and the black. Then he donned his acangatara headdress of feathers, and went around to see how everybody was. They were all astonished to see him dressed up in so much festive paint, because today was not a festive day, except for the man who had taken over his wife's birthpangs so that she would not suffer. He had groaned in his hammock, suffering the most appalling cramps and contractions for four days so that his wife could give birth as usual after a few minutes squatting over a hole in the ground. But it was a festive day for him today, because today he felt better, and was able to eat an entire haruzam toad for breakfast.

Anane went to check his bananas, his maize and his groundnuts, but there was nothing to do except pull off some weeds, so he went and watched the women making chicha by spitting the chewed wads into a fermenting bowl, and he watched the women who were grinding manioc and singing

'Cuddle Up a Little Closer, Lovely Mine', which had been handed down amongst the people ever since the days of Maharon, when the only explorers who had ever escaped had taught it to them before escaping. Humming the tune, he went to ask when it would be that the adolescent girls would be ready to come out of their huts and start being women, but nobody knew exactly, since they had only been sitting in the dark for a couple of months with their hair over their faces, and it was still too early to question them since they had to be spared even the shock of being asked questions about how they were. Anane went down to the river for another bath, even though it would take off a lot of his pigments, because he had the idea that the *bufea* that was swimming there wanted to tell him something.

When Anane came out again he went to ask his wife to ask her mother if he could exchange the hammock she had made for two scarlet macaws that he had captive, and who grew good feathers for decorations, and his mother-in-law told his wife that she wanted three macaws, and so he agreed, and his wife had to go back to her mother again to say that it was settled. Anane was pleased, and never questioned once the tabu against talking to one's wife's mother. His wife whispered something in his ear that made him smile, and she took him into the forest where they did toke-toke together because it was good and because she wanted another child. In the forest he told her that the *bufea* in the river wanted to mate with him and have a dolphin-child, and she said yes, but he was not to disappear with the dolphin for ever like so many others who found the ecstasy so great that they failed to notice that they were drowning until they floated away with dead eyes, but with a joyful smile and a stream of tiny bubbles rising from their mouths, to be stripped by caimans and piranhas, so that the other tribes would find only their thigh-bones and make them into flutes whose bell-like notes could call dolphins from afar out of the curiosity and the melancholy of regret. Anane said that he would be careful, and then they came back and dug a candiru fish out of the wet sand where they had buried it yesterday to keep it fresh until today. They roasted it in the embers and tore off half each, throwing the bones where the birds and animals could squabble for them, but keeping the jaws with their teeth that were so good for surgery and for extracting jiggers from the flesh.

Anane went down to the river for his third bath, and the *bufea* came against him and brushed him with her rubbery smooth flesh, nudging him with her long snout and provoking him into flirtation, so that they rolled together in the water. Coupled together, the *bufea* sang out beneath the ringing water and flipped with her tail in short sweeps so that the paje Anane knew all at once why it was that so many died by mistake simply because the loving dolphins tried so hard to give pleasure. Anane reminded himself to breathe every time they rolled to the surface; he reminded himself to keep up a pressure on his nostrils so that he did not breathe in the water which was so fresh from the mountains that it was infinitely more intoxicating than the air. When they had finished, and they were returning from the bliss of their submarine delirium, he held on about the flexible neck of the *bufea*, and she swam to the place where she would leave upon the sandbar their child, Rebu.

Rebu grew up amongst the Navantes much as Venu had grown up amongst the cabocos, except that he had a father in Anane, and another father who was almost a father in Aurelio, and he had a mother who was a *bufea* who swam in the river, and a mother who was almost a mother in Anane's wife. He learned how to wrestle with the men and play music in the men's hut, except that he could play the flute just by using his own voice. He learned how to make toy arrows that whistled like a dolphin because at the tips would be fastened the shells of nuts, and he learned that because his eyes were of different colours, he was a dolphin man who would one day swim away for ever.

Rebu swam away when he was ten years old, without knowing where it was that he was going. In the water he lost much of his human nature and all his memories, because his nature was confused and ambivalent, and for a while he lost much of his power of sight, since it was more use in the water to sing out and listen to the sounds that reverberated so much more clearly than the light shone in the dappled darkness. When they found him and took him in, he was exhausted and half-starved, lying on a sandbank ringed by caimans who were cautiously waiting for him to die because they did not know what kind of food he was.

Venezia first knew about Roberto when she was walking down the Calle Bolivar. Roberto was singing to himself in a pitch so high that only someone like Venezia could have heard it. It was a melody so alien and so plaintive that Venezia was reminded of the time when her name had been different to what it was now, but also somehow similar. She thought that she knew how the melody continued, and as she walked towards the river where Roberto was sitting on the bank watching the water that had once died because of the miners' mercury, she joined in the song so that suddenly Roberto's melody changed to a joyful one, and he joined in with her joining in with him.

Venezia, eighteen years old, and as tawny-skinned as Amadea her mother, broke into a run and allowed the contents of her *muchilla* to spill over the road and be danced upon by the dust-devils. When she arrived at the river she came straight upon Roberto, eighteen years old also, golden-skinned, with eyes of different colours, who had already stood up and turned around in order to be ready to greet her.

Confronted by each other, the two young people could not think of a word to say. Roberto smiled upon her with the same speechless smile as Amadea's lover had worn upon the day when he had held out his hand offering the quintessence of earth. He held out his hand to her just as the dolphin had. Venezia smiled at him in return, and shrugged her shoulders as if to say that nothing could be said. She took his proffered hand, and they sat down on the ground opposite each other.

Roberto intended to invite her to accompany him to the feria on Saturday, but when he looked into her eyes, he was unable to look away or to speak, because he felt that he was submerged by them. She looked back into his eyes and felt the same.

Lost in each other's mesmerising gaze, still holding hands, at first they were engulfed by nothingness, a kind of blackness that receded into the distance without ever diminishing, and then they began to see what neither of them had seen for a very long time. Roberto looked into her brown eyes and saw parakeets, and she looked into his and saw a piraruca swimming in the depths. He saw howler monkeys, and she saw green macaws. He saw sandbars and rubber trees, and she saw cashews and quebrachos, herons and canoes.

Their vision blurred and was obscured by water. There was broken light refracted from above, and there were murky shapes dimly shifting, but instead of light there was now music.

The crowd of people who gathered around in astonished curiosity said that they were singing to each other for a very long time, and that for long stretches patches of the melody seemed to be missing. They reported that they had never seen upon human faces expressions of such extraordinary beatitude, and that it was like the joy of reunited lovers after a long period of separation caused by disapproving families. They stated that the melody was quite unlike any other melody that they had ever heard, that it was an aquatic melody that smelled of trees and roots and nuts sprouting in sodden ground, that it was like flutes, and bells tolling in submerged lakes in the bell towers of inundated churches. They said that it was a very long time before any of them had realised that the couple had died upright, holding hands and gazing into each other's eyes, because the reverie induced by the spell of their duet lasted long after it was finished. The Alcalde of Chiriguana declared upon the Certificates of Death that they had died of sublimity, because even though he was a venial man who kept goats in the kitchen and had sold his own niece to the grocer, he had the soul of a poet who had sometimes recognised intimations of the ineffable in his own life. When they were buried together by the banks of the Mula, he said in his oration that he knew from the evidence all about the lethality of visions of perfect beauty, and of everything else connected with the remembrance of paradise.

THE MAN WHO SENT TWO DEAD FISH TO THE PRESIDENT

There seems to be no escape from people called 'Joao'. It is not just that in Brazilian novels the hero is always called 'Joao' and that many of the authors seem to have that name as well, it is also the case that in some places no man seems to have any other name, so that one has to qualify one's references with helpful additions, such as 'You know, the one who got bitten by an alligator' or 'Joao who fell in love with the transvestite in Rio, and didn't discover the truth until they went to bed'. Anyone who has ever been to the Island of Kerkire and discovered that all the men are called 'Spiro' will understand what I mean by saying that the name 'Joao' has a kind of tiresome inevitability about it that makes one feel a deep weariness.

It is therefore with an implicit apology that I have to admit that this story is about Joao, the one who lived next to the river and had a gift for veridical dreams.

He lived in a wooden hut on stilts that was designed to keep him dry in the rainy season when the waters rose dramatically in minutes and stayed that way for months until they began to recede almost as swiftly. Ever since the logging had begun he had been having difficulties because stray logs would float down the river and knock against the stilts of the hut.

One day he had awoken at dawn to find that he had managed to sleep through a collision that had left his hut at an angle of forty-five degrees. He had had to leave it that way until the waters went down and he could sink new piles into the forest floor. As an afterthought he had built a strong palisade to keep errant logs away in the future. He had noticed that over the years the floods had been getting more violent and the waters more stained, which was because the trees that used to transpire the water and break its flow were no longer there, and the top-soil of the cattle farms was simply being carried away to the sea, leaving the land perpetually useless.

Like many people of his name, Joao was a very large and hairy individual who would have reminded people of a bear, if they had ever seen a picture of one. His chest was phenomenal in circumference, and beneath it there hung a capacious belly as rounded as a tumulus and as tight as a drum. His legs were rem-iniscent of temple pillars, and so hirsute that when he emerged from the water after catching turtles, it looked as though he had a three-toed sloth hanging from either side of his torso in place of the usual ambulatory apparatus. He had a round and flat face adorned with a wild black beard that could never be brought to order, through which could be discerned a sensual pair of lips and an oddly plump nose, so marked with blackheads that it looked like a lump of pale pumice. His eyes were ebony brown, and had the habit of flickering from side to side when he spoke, an effect that other people found hypnotic and very attractive. It seems that he had never learned that most people when they converse fix their gaze on only one eye of their interlocutor, and so he skipped from one eye to the other, as though he were rum-maging in the other's soul for an interpretation of their psyche.

Joao lived a life of the simplest subsistence, which meant that for most of the time he did very little. He spent a lot of the time swinging in his hammock, swatting mosquitoes and sandflies, indulging in reveries, having fantasies about all the women he had had and that he was going to have, and gilding their images so that the reality would always be somehow less real than he had imagined. Joao was rather like a cat in that he had mastered the art of doing absolutely nothing without ever being bored, an art largely lost in more civilised climes. Much of the time he made plans in his head of all the things that he was going to do one day, and this frequently gave him the comfortable feeling that he had already accomplished them. He had a dream about going to Rio, for example, where the women are obsessed with the shape of their bodies and prance around virtually naked at carnival, where everybody gets so drunk that the streets run with piss for days at a time. He had a dream about going to the goldmines and making a fortune, but he also knew that really no one ever did, and that the miners always ended up with mercury poisoning, and syphilis from the overworked camp whores. The thought of making a fortune was much pleasanter than actually having to go out and drudge for it, as far as he was concerned. It was much easier to loll in his hammock in between going out in his canoe to catch fish with fish-fuddle or a line, or to stroll through the dry bits looking for capybara to roast and fruits to cram his belly with.

Joao was between women. His last woman had been carried away by an inexplicable fever about a year ago. He had loved her very much, so much that whilst he was with her the thought of sleeping with anyone else had been absolutely repulsive. This emotion was so unfamiliar to him that he was not only perpetually astonished by it, but was also convinced that it was in the nature of a personal message from God about the purpose of life and the meaning of love. His wife had been a small, lively woman, a mestiza who had been genetically concocted out of every possible race, and was therefore gifted with the intelligence and beauty characteristic of all such people. Joao had come out more like a white man than anything else, even though his father was black and his mother was mostly Indian, and sometimes he felt inferior to his wife, who seemed to embody more of the wide world than he did.

Joao and his wife never had any children, which used to upset her a little, but which secretly pleased Joao because he wanted to devote his time to her exclusively and learn to relish the intensity of his love. Like most people who do very little Joao and his wife had plenty of energy for lovemaking, and there was no more delicious pleasure than to make love in the rainy season with the rain hammering relentlessly on the corrugated iron, go blissfully to sleep, and then wake up after who knows how long to make love all over again. Joao and his wife used to feel that they had been unaccountably blessed.

Then she had gone down with the fever. It started with a dreadful shivering and trembling, and she could not tell whether she was freezing cold or desperately hot because she was both at once and by turns. Then she began to feel appallingly tired, as though she had been weighted down with hunks of lead. She took to her hammock, but could not stay there because she was struck with a flux. The diarrhoea became so bad that in the end she was perpetually flowing with water and blood and was seized by excruciating stomach cramps that made her cry out and clutch at her husband's arm, so that after she died he still had the marks of her fingernails in his flesh. She seemed to wither away before his eyes. Her skin became like dried leaves and hung about her bones like a sallow fabric. Her hair started to come out, and in the end she could not move, being forced to lie in the midst of her own bloody excrement. Joao cleaned her up the whole time, with tears flowing down his cheeks and soaking his beard as he addressed angry prayers to God and all the saints, the Virgin, and all the black-magic gods and goddesses as well. He threatened Exu the pitchfork demon with dire consequences if he did not remove the evil curse from his wife, and even made a doll of Exu and stuck his knife through its heart. Most people would not have dared to do such a foolhardy thing to Exu, but Joao was desperate, and also confident of his own spiritual power. Possibly Exu forgave him, knowing that the disease was really caused by the untreated sewage pumped into the river miles upstream at the new logging settlement. Long after his wife died, telling him in her last breath that she would love him for ever, Joao discovered that he should have treated her with a solution of salt and sugar, and he cursed himself for his ignorance. He thought that if he had learned to read and write, then she would not have died.

Joao went to the primary school and joined the little children in the class. He was like a mountainous child amongst the little ones, repeating the alphabet, reciting from the board sentences about Lucho the Mountain Lion leaving his lumps of sugar lying on the lino, the United States is the richest country in the world, Juanito the jaguar jumps into the jungle, Bahia is where all the cacao came from, Ribeiro the writer writes about whales. Like the little children Joao frequently burst into tears, except that in his case it was not over who stole my ruler and who pinched me when you weren't looking, miss, it was about his wife disintegrating and disappearing before his eyes, and it was about having been thrown out of the garden of love with no prospect of re-entering it. The tears frothed up from the cavernous emptiness of his stomach and the constricted ventricles of his heart, and the young teacher from Sao Paulo doing her bit for the ignorant of the interior would find herself as often putting her arm around him to shush him as she did with the little ones. She became used to finding her shirt soaked with his convulsive sobs, and philosophising with him after school about how time can heal and about how one should be grateful for what life gives and resigned about what it takes away. She was filled with admiration for the strength of his love and the rapidity of his learning, and it will surprise no one that eventually this young and idealistic middle-class girl fell in love with the bear of the backwoods and rekindled his happiness. But that is another story, and is nothing to do with how he came to send two dead fish to the President of the United States.

After his wife died Joao was in a state of shock that must have jerked something open in his mind. Apart from the feeling of his wife's palpable presence and his feeling that he could continue to converse with her about no matter what, Joao began to have dreams at night. He did not tell anyone about it because he did not want to acquire the reputation of a sorcerer, but he dreamed very clearly that there were going to be free elections in Brazil just a week before they were announced and that they were going to be chaotic. He dreamed that Paulo was going to cut himself on the leg with a machete, and in fact Paulo cut his hand with a knife, which was nearly right. He dreamed that a macaw told him that Macunaima the Hero Emperor of the Virgin Backwoods was in the area, and later on he saw in the forest a strange man with only one leg being followed by flocks of macaws.

One morning Joao had a very vivid dream just before waking. The dream was that two mighty tyrants had fallen and that the whole course of history was about to change. He awoke with the feeling that this was a mightily important dream, and for once he decided that he had to tell someone. If history was about to change it was obvious that the powerful and important people of the world ought to be informed of it so that they could plan in advance as to the best way of coping with it. He knew from school that the two most powerful countries in the world were the United States and the USSR, and his first thought was that the leaders of these two countries ought to know about his dream.

But after he had awoken properly, eaten some cassava, and thought about it all over again, it occurred to him that perhaps his dream might have been a false one, like the one he had had about the earth crashing into the moon on St Esteban's Day. Joao did not want to make a fool of himself by informing the most powerful people in the world of something that had not happened, and he thought that perhaps it would be better if he kept his peace and let them discover it for themselves, if it had happened.

But when he went down the ladder to go fishing, he discovered that washed up on the bank were two dead fish in perfect condition. One was an arowhana, the kind that looks after its babies in its mouth and leaps out of the water to pick beetles from overhanging branches, and the other was a tucunare with a false eye on its tail so that other fish would think that it was swimming backwards and get confused.

Joao bent down and picked them up, one in each hand. He thought that really this was too much of a coincidence. He was very happy to have such incontestable evidence of the truth of his dream, and he resolved not only to inform the leaders of the USA and the USSR, but to send them the evidence as well.

But this gave him a problem, because he realised that he could not send two fish to each president, since that would be four fish altogether. He thought of killing two more fish, and perhaps sending one true fish to each president with one false one each. But then he thought that they might have very clever people who could tell the difference, and he thought that maybe that would damage his credibility, so Joao decided to send them both to the President of the United States, with a request that he should pass the information on to the other president.

Joao built a small fire with dry wood, and when it was well established he piled it with damp wood and aromatic leaves. He hung the two fish above the smoke, and revisited the fire at regular intervals to check that it was still good and smoky. He sniffed at the air and listened for the croaking of the frogs in order to check that it was not going to rain, and took a piece of dried palm up into his hut. He wrote: 'Dear Gringo Presedent. I want to tell you that two tirants have fallen, wich is very impootant. Please tell the Presedent of the ussristos. Here are two fish wich are prufe. respecfully, Joao.'

When the fish were well smoked, had turned brown and shrivelled the correct amount, Joao rubbed them with salt, put salt in their mouths, and wrapped them tightly in palm leaves, enclosing his letter, and then tied the bundle with creeper.

THE DEPOSIT

It was the spring of 1982, and there was a war going on in the Falkland Islands. The whole nation was abuzz with it. In parliament the usual disconnected idealists were trying to kid themselves and every one else that United Nations diplomacy could solve the problem, and others were muttering about how diplomacy hadn't been of any use in dealing with Hitler. Lord Carrington had resigned, the word 'Exocet' had suddenly entered into common parlance, hideous personal tragedies were in the process of unfolding, the Argentine dictatorship was about to collapse, and Mrs Thatcher and her government were about to glory in their finest hour.

All of this was of no consequence to the tall young man who walked unsteadily, his eyes blinking rapidly and the right side of his face twitching. A junkie feels no hunger, but he was nonetheless dizzy with lack of food, not just because he had been travelling for two days without eating, but also because for many months the buying of sustenance had had to take second place to the acquisition of the white powder without which he could no longer function.

It was astonishing how quickly his descent into dependency had occurred. Other people seemed to be able to shoot up once or twice, experience the bliss of the rush, and then never take heroin again. They could mention it in conversation, and everyone would be impressed by how cool they were, asking them things like 'But weren't you scared of getting addicted?' whereupon they would reply, 'Well, I felt terrible afterwards for quite a while. I mean, I can't tell you how terrible you feel, and I thought of taking some more, but then I thought, "Hey, don't be stupid, you've done it and now you don't have to do it again."'

In Michael Henchard's case, however, the bliss had been so paradisiacal, and the subsequent descent into hell so abysmal, that he had realised straight away that he would have to go out and score some more. Simultaneously, and without any apparent awareness of the contradiction, he had managed to persuade himself that of course he would be able to stop at any time, he could be cool about it when he had to jack it in.

It was easy to score in Christminster, but it was impossible to continue to be a student there. You can't study music at such a high level when you're either stoned and in heaven or desperate with craving, being sick, hallucinating and having diarrhoea. He had spent all his grant money, he had shoplifted, he had raided the wallets of friends, he had stolen from his parents. He had even sold the carriage clock that had come down the family for generations, and the silver plate given to his father by his brother officers on the occasion of his wedding in 1953. The worst thing he did was to persuade his girlfriend, Susan, to try it, and when she'd got to like being stoned, he persuaded her to sleep with the dealer in return for another bag. Then Susan went off with the dealer because she'd got completely hooked, and that way she could get high for free, at least until he tired of her and sold her on to a pimp.

It was music that kept him going for a while. He had a very fine old violin, and a very great talent, and there was a hinterland between being stoned and being in hell that was just wide enough for him to be able to busk on Marygreen Street, outside one of the famous colleges. Here there would be Japanese and American tourists who had come to experience the atmosphere of the medieval buildings of that famous centre of learning, and here there would be enough young students from rich families, who might toss coins into his open violin case. He was fortunate that he was such a good player, because otherwise the police would have moved him on more often than they did. His appearance had become wild, and he was filthy and emaciated, his speech had degenerated into an ersatz and inarticulate transatlantic patois, but he played like an angel, and this was often enough to extenuate the officiousness even of the Christminster police.

At night he slept behind the dustbins at the entrance to the underground car park near the Beaumont Hotel, wrapped up in a rug he had stolen from a car, hugging his violin tightly to his chest because his junkie friends knew it was valuable, and none of them, however much they liked him, would have hesitated for one moment to steal it if the opportunity had arisen.

Finally he had been forced to leave Christminster altogether, because the friend who had originally given him his first high for nothing had inevitably become his supplier, and now he owed him a stupendous amount of money. He had been cornered down at his little patch behind the dustbins, and the dealer's thugs had given him such a good kicking that he had been doubled up with pain for two days, almost unable to move. One of his front teeth had gone, he had a split lip, and he was sure that he had cracked some ribs. It was an effort to breathe. He was glad that he had had the presence of mind to hide the violin in a dustbin as soon as he heard the noise of footsteps coming down the ramp of the car park so late at night. They would have taken it, without a doubt, and quite probably they would have smashed it.

Nonetheless, Michael Henchard had gone to his dealer to plead for one more day to pay, and for one more bag of smack, because he didn't have any more, and if he didn't have any, then how was he going to get his head together to go out and find the dough?

It was after obtaining an extension of his debt and one more bag of smack that Michael Henchard took to the road. He left Christminster and walked all the way down Abingdon Road until he reached the roundabout on the southern bypass. He had no idea where he was going. He was fortunate that there were so many music lovers who drove cars, because more often than not it was the sight of the violin case slung over his shoulder that made motorists think that they could trust him, despite his miserable appearance. There were post-hippy types, too, with flowers brightly painted on the doors and roofs of their yellow Volkswagen Beetles and their Renault 4s, who would assume that he might be, 'Like, in a band, or something cool like that, man'.

On the first day, which included many hours of waiting in the rain at the roadside whilst respectable people whizzed past, he managed to travel down the A34 to Wintoncester, where he spent a night in a bus shelter with a garrulous alcoholic. On the second day he went along the A272 and the A30 to Melchester, and from there he got a lift with an inexplicably charitable and respectable old lady in a venerable Singer Gazelle, who took him down the A354 to Casterbridge. All the way she talked at high speed and with complete inconsequence about the many relatives of hers who were acquainted with various baronets, deans and bishops, and did not notice that her passenger was white-faced and black-eyed with torment in the back.

She pressed a one-pound note into his hands, and left him at Grey's Bridge, where he read a bronze plaque set into the stones, that quaintly threatened deportation for anyone who wilfully damaged it, and then he set off up the hill into the town. He had decided that he would not take his last dose of smack until he reached the centre. Such arbitrary targets are routinely set, such decisions routinely made, and as routinely broken, by addicts of all complexions.

He could tell that it was a beautiful old town, even though beauty in all its forms had recently become all but imperceptible to him. Ancient buildings lined the long hill of High East Street, and there was something gentle and consolatory about the way that the houses had settled into their foundations as if enjoying a nap after lunch. Outside a newsagent's he saw a stand with a poster for the *Sun* newspaper on it, which read 'GOTCHA!' and he wondered briefly what it meant.

Unsure of where he was going or what he intended to do, he crossed over Top o'Town roundabout, and had begun to walk along the Port Bredy Road, when he realised that he had come too far. He turned around and retraced his steps, not even noticing the large bronze monument on his left.

What he did notice, however, was a small shop on his right, with 'Farfrae's Music' painted above the window in Gothic script. In days past he would have been thrilled to have come across it. He would have gone in, regardless of the protests of whomever he was with, and he would have rifled through the violin section looking for duets. He would have wanted to know what kind of rosin was in stock, and whether or not there were interesting kinds of strings. He would have tried out every violin there, even though he had never in his life come across anything better than the one he had, and no one these days stocked anything except student ones from China. An initially truculent shopkeeper would inevitably have been won over by the extraordinary cantabile tone that the boy could produce even on the cheapest instrument.

Now, however, Michael Henchard was thinking only about getting enough money to score another hit after he had used the one that was left. He had no idea where he could score, but junkies who find themselves in strange places, like homosexuals who can detect others just by the look in someone's eyes, seem to have an instinct. He would go into the Three Mariners or the Greyhound Inn, and he would spot someone in the corner of a public bar, someone who looked out of place, someone marginal, and there would be a moment of recognition. Even if that person wasn't a junkie themselves, they would know someone who was. Maybe there would be someone loitering in a dark street for no apparent purpose. The most important thing was to find the money first, and then he could work out a way to get the smack.

Behind the counter of Farfrae's Music was a young man in his mid-twenties, with a handlebar moustache, and golden hair that was brushed across his forehead and came down to the collar of his cheerful pink shirt. Donald Farfrae had the most musical of Scottish accents, from somewhere outside

Edinburgh, and he knew many a sad Scottish ballad, which he could render in an expressive tenor voice. Every teenage girl in Casterbridge had a crush on him, some of them even taking up an instrument so as to have an excuse to while away the time in his shop. They would notice how his forehead shone when the light caught it, and how nicely his hair was cut, and the sort of velvet pile or down that was on the skin at the back of his neck, and how his cheek was so truly curved as to be part of a globe, and how clearly drawn were the lids and lashes which hid his grey eyes. When Michael Henchard entered the shop, Donald Farfrae was singing to himself, 'It's hame, and it's hame, hame fain would I be, O hame, hame, hame, to my ain countree—' He stopped abruptly, however, when he saw Henchard.

No one would have been pleased to find Michael Henchard walking into an otherwise empty shop where they were the sole member of staff. It was bad enough getting alcoholics and the occasional tramp, but even so, none of these were as dreadful as some of the local music teachers. Not even the music teachers, however, could have been as bad as Michael Henchard, who was not only filthy, bedraggled, toggle-haired, cadaverous and wild-eyed, but also had about him an unpredictable air of violence, or even madness.

'Can I help you at all?' asked Farfrae, determined to remain cool, and make the best of it.

'It's this, man,' said Henchard, placing the violin case on the counter.

'What about it, sir? How can I be of assistance?' Farfrae fervently wished that Henchard would just go away. He sometimes got characters like this in the shop, who, like malfunctioning satellites, were more or less lost and disorientated on the way to Glastonbury. They invariably talked in fake American accents. You could tell the junkies because they could hardly keep their eyes open, they were always in a dreadful state of health, they often smelled repulsive, and they could speak only in languid monotones. They normally bought a plectrum, or one top E string for a folk guitar. He noticed that Henchard had rows of festering scabs on his forearms. 'O shit,' he thought.

'I'm selling it, man. You buying?'

'Let's take a look,' said Farfrae, and he opened the case. Farfrae was himself a pianist, but he had been interested in instruments of all kinds for quite long enough to be able to recognise a superior violin. It was strongly constructed, largely proportioned, but not at all clumsy or heavy. The scroll was a perfect imitation of a Stradivarius, as indeed, now he came to think of it, was the entire violin. It had margins that were full and strong, and the purfling was executed with perfect elegance. On the back the sycamore was wonderfully marked, with a dark yellow varnish in the middle that graduated to a deep ruby red in the hollows.

Farfrae looked inside to try to discern a maker's label, and there was indeed one there, but it was too filthy to be legible. 'How much do you want for it?' he asked, and Henchard swayed on his feet and made a meaningless gesture with his left hand.

'Like, I dunno, man, I mean, like ... fifty?'

'Fifty?' repeated Farfrae incredulously.

'Yeah, well, like, if it's too much ...' said Henchard.

'I think it's worth a lot more than fifty,' said Farfrae, who was struggling with his conscience, and had already won a small battle. He was one of those people who naturally find dishonesty too much of a strain.

'Well, man, whatever,' said Henchard.

'How do I know it's yours? I can't accept stolen goods, or even goods which might be. Do you have provenance for it?'

Henchard blinked and tried hard to concentrate. 'Well, like, it was passed down, and we always had it, you know? There was this story ... . there was ... I mean, it was sold to one of my great-grandads, or great-great or whatever, and the dude who sold it ... he was like ... I mean, he won it as a prize or something. At the conservatoire, man.'

'The Paris Conservatoire?'

'Hey ...' said Henchard, shrugging his shoulders.

'How do I know it's yours, though?'

'Jesus,' protested Henchard. 'All these questions.' He picked up the bow, and tightened the horsehair. He opened the little compartment in the case which was situated under the neck of the instrument, and took out a lump of rosin, which he stroked a couple of times along the hairs. He laid the bow down and took up the violin. He tuned the three lower strings deftly with a few exact movements of the pegs, tuned the E string with the micro-adjuster, and put the instrument to his chin. He tapped the strings a couple of times with the bow, to check that he had the right tension on the hairs, held a momentary pose, and began to play.

Farfrae watched and listened, utterly amazed, because a miracle was taking place before his eyes, in his own shop. It was a simple little piece in C, allegro moderato, consisting of four clusters of semiquavers to a bar. It was very regular, and there was nothing very surprising in it, but it was extraordinarily pretty in the hands of the ragged young man, who was now altering the pattern of the piece by inserting all kinds of unpredictable slurs and staccatos. He reached the final jump from the last C of the second beat of the last bar, and brought it down smartly to the final minim C an octave below. He ended the note with absolute precision, and looked up at Farfrae. 'Kreutzer etude number two, man,' he said, 'like, just to warm up, you know. With improvements I kinda just made up.'

'That violin,' said Farfrae disbelievingly, 'the tone is unbelievable. It's like silver, or gold, or ... I'm gobsmacked, I really am.'

'You're Scottish,' said Henchard, and he tucked the violin under his chin again, and tore through 'Up Tails A', skipping across two strings at a time, and making it sound as if it had been written by Arcangelo Corelli. Then he launched into the Hungarian March from *The Damnation of Faust*, executing the high Bs and As with astonishing clarity and distinctness. Even more remarkable than this display of musicianship was the transformation of the player as he played. He swayed a little, his eyes closed, and Farfrae really thought he looked as though he had been possessed by an angel.

'OK, I believe it's yours,' he said, 'but really you shouldn't sell it. You're too good.'

'Please, man,' said Henchard. 'I mean, like, really please. I'll take fifty.' He put the violin back into its case, detensioned the bow, and returned it to the case as well. 'Fifty,' he repeated, and looked up pleadingly.

Farfrae resolved the terrible quandary within himself: 'I'll give you fifty, but it's only a deposit. I'm going to get it valued, and when you come back we'll talk about it again, and either I can pay you the rest or, if you want it back, all you've got to do is give me back the fifty pounds, OK?'

'Whatever,' said Henchard. 'I just need, you know, like, the dough, man, that's all.'

Farfrae opened the till and took out fifty pounds in ten-pound notes. 'What might your name be?' he asked, and then he found his receipt book, opened it up and wrote, 'To Michael Henchard, the sum of fifty pounds in consideration of Stradivarius pattern violin. 3/5/82.' He tore the receipt out of the book, and tried to give it to Henchard, who did not respond, so he reached out and tucked it into his shirt pocket. Then he handed over the fifty pounds.

Henchard took it, and lurched away towards the door. When he reached it, he turned and waved loosely, clutching the notes in his fingers. 'Thanks, man,' he said, 'but, like … today, you know … it's a really really bad day.'

With a leaden heart, and tears in his eyes, knowing that he was a traitor to himself but unable to do anything about it, Henchard went out into the street and began to wander down the hill. Dejected and bereft, he sat at the foot of the statue of William Barnes, enduring the hostile and suspicious glances of passers-by, and waited until after dark. Then he went and crouched in a doorway near a dim street lamp in Grey School Passage, where he prepared his gear, drew a tourniquet round his arm, and injected his last dose. It was a larger hit than usual, and he realised almost straight away that it was bad stuff. The vengeful dealer had written off his debts with a malicious cut. Michael Henchard was half dead at midnight by the stone post in the middle of Bull Stake Square, and he was lucky that an insomniac found him when they were out walking the dog.

In January of 2003, approximately twenty-one years later, a tall and rubicund man in his forties called in on Farfrae's Music, coming in out of the snow, and stamping his feet good-humouredly. He had about him an air of prosperity. At his side was a woman about ten years his junior, whose hand was being tightly held by a little girl of about six, who was wrapped up in a scarf and coat, and wore a Bugs Bunny hat with rabbit's ears upon her head.

Outside the newsagent's, a *Sun* poster said something like, 'GO GET 'IM, TONE!' Everyone was talking about the possibility of a new war in Iraq, with the intention of deposing Saddam Hussein, and the usual people were making the usual predictable points in the media about the United Nations, and the value or otherwise of unilateral action. The man who had just entered Frafrae's shop, however, was thinking of no such thing.

Behind the counter stood Donald Farfrae, singing to himself, ' ... When the flower is in the bud, and the leaf upon the tree, The lark shall sing me hame to my ain countree.' He was moustacheless and bespectacled these days, his golden hair, much shorter and thinner, was subdued by specklings of grey. He had lost none of his Scottish charm, and nowadays it was women aged twenty-eight and above who took up musical instruments so they had good reason to dawdle in his shop. As far as he was concerned this was a distinct improvement on schoolgirls that he wasn't allowed to touch at all. 'Can I help you?' he asked.

'Well, I don't know, I certainly hope so,' said the customer. He drew from his wallet a very old slip of paper, very grubby, much crumpled, and handed it over. 'Do you remember anything about this?' he asked.

Farfrae looked at it for a moment, and then said simply, 'Good God.'

'Do you remember anything? Was it you that I spoke to?'

'The violin! Good God, the violin! Yes, indeed! Indeed, it was me. But how you've changed! I never would have recognised you.'

'I did sell it to you, didn't I? Something's been tweaking at my memory, and it's really been bothering me. You may recall the state I was in. I was on my last legs, and that night I really overdid it. I suppose you realised that I was, um … you know, an addict … a junkie? After I left you I nearly killed myself, by accident, I mean, and it's just lucky that I was found in time.'

'Well, sir, I had my suspicions. As you say, you were in a state. But I've never forgotten the noise you made when you played. One of the highlights of my musical life, I would say. I do hope you still play, sir, it would be criminal not to.'

'It's very kind of you to say so. I can't imagine it can have been very good. I do play. It took me a very long time to get back on course, but I made it in the end, I swore off the stuff and eventually I managed to put everything back together, except that I didn't have the violin. The one I have now was lent to me by a Japanese foundation.'

He paused, and Donald Farfrae exclaimed, 'Of course! You're Michael Henchard! The Michael Henchard! I saw you last year, with the Bournemouth Symphony Orchestra! You were doing the Bruch and the Walton. Well, well, well. I must say, it was marvellous. I'd say that times have certainly changed for you since you last entered these doors, that's for sure.'

Henchard ignored these comments. 'You sold it eventually, I suppose? I mean, I'm not asking for it back. I just wondered what happened to it. Recently I've been thinking about it, and as we were staying nearby, I thought I'd come in on the off chance.'

'Well, sir,' said Farfrae, much excited, 'I took it to my friend Colin in Chalk Newton. He did all my repairs – he still does, in fact – and he knows a lot about violins. He said it was the most perfect imitation of a Strad he'd ever seen. He played it a bit and said it was something really special, so he took it to Hill's, in London.'

'You're not telling me it was a Strad, are you? Aren't they all accounted for?'

'No, sir, it was a Lupot. There was a label inside that they managed to decipher, and then it was obvious from everything else that it was original. It said, "N. Lupot. Luthier de la Musique du Roi et de l'Ecole Royale de Musique, Paris 1820." You see, I even memorised it. It explains a lot: why it was so beautiful, why it sounded so perfect.'

'Oh God, it was a Lupot,' said Michael Henchard, 'and I promised my father I would never part with it. We'd had it so long. For generations.' He looked at Farfrae. 'He died last year, and he never really forgave me for it, though God knows I've done worse things. I can't believe it was a Lupot. I'd kill to have a Lupot. All the violinists I know would kill to have one, even if it was just for chamber music. There's a story that Spohr even preferred his to his Strad and his Guarnerius. And Reményi used to soft-talk his, as if it was his mistress. Everyone loves them.'

'You don't have to go out and kill for one, sir,' said Donald Farfrae, his voice brimming with pleasure. 'Obviously we couldn't sell it. I can't tell you what arguments and discussions we had about it. It was worth hundreds of thousands, but it was really quite plain all the time that we couldn't sell it. Quite apart from the question of provenance, there was the simple fact that I hadn't bought it.'

'You didn't buy it?'

'No, sir.' He waved the receipt. 'I gave you fifty pounds as a deposit. This isn't a receipt for a sale, it records that I gave you a deposit. I never put a time limit on your return, which was perhaps stupid of me, but there you are, it's too late now. Colin's had the violin all this time, safely under lock and key. I'll draw you a map to get to his workshop, it's not far, and I'll phone him and tell him you're coming. I know he's there because I just spoke to him.'

His hands trembling with excitement, but perhaps with some regret in his heart, he drew a map that directed Michael Henchard northwards from the Top o'Town roundabout, past the statue of Thomas Hardy.

'I can't tell you how much this means to me,' said Henchard, as he took the piece of paper. 'I'll never forget this, and I'll be grateful till the day I die, I can promise you. The most amazing thing is that you could have sold it for a fortune, and you didn't.'

Farfrae shrugged. 'It's not my style,' he said, 'ducking and diving. Altogether too much bother.'

As Henchard reached the door, Farfrae said, 'Aren't you forgetting something, sir?'

'Am I?'

'You owe me fifty pounds. If you take the violin back, you have to return my deposit.'

'Oh, quite right,' said Henchard, much amused. He took his wallet out of his pocket and counted it out, all in ten-pound notes.

'Oh, and one more thing,' said Farfrae. 'Would you be so kind as to come back here with it and play that Kreutzer etude for me? I never forgot it, how wonderfully you played it.'

'The Kreutzer Number Two? Well, of course, but wouldn't you like something a bit more sophisticated? I learned that when I was twelve. '

'No, sir,' said Donald Farfrae, 'I would not like anything else.'

'It's funny how everybody loves to hear you play that,' said Henchard's wife, speaking now for the first time. She turned to Farfrae. 'It was hearing him play it that made me fall for him in the first place. He was warming up before a concert, and I was waiting for him to stop so that I could get some practice in myself. It made me feel that an angel had got inside him. God knows, there wasn't much else to recommend him.'

'I can play it, too,' announced the little girl, 'and I'm only six.'

'This precocious little rabbit is Elizabeth Jane,' said Henchard, squeezing her shoulder. 'She's got a quarter size, and she's not bad at all.'

'Hello, Rabbit,' said Farfrae.

Henchard turned to his wife, saying, 'Let's go to Chalk Newton for a touching reunion. And on the way back we'll pick up a case of champagne for Mr Farfrae here.'

'To be perfectly honest, I'd greatly prefer Scotch,' said Farfrae.

'Whisky it is, then. I'll get you some nice single malt.'

Farfrae laughed, and said drily, 'Well, as long as you don't go thinking it's a deposit you can come back for. I don't think I'll be hanging on to it for twenty years, and in this case I don't think I'd agree to be parted from it.'

ANDOUIL AND ANDOUILLETTE BEGIN THEIR HOLIDAY

To those who know her, Madame Andouil is fondly nicknamed 'Andouillette'. This diminutive feminisation of her husband's surname was so obvious a notion that very soon after her marriage she had ceased to resent it, even though the name denotes a type of sausage that she considers particularly odious, with its offcuts of intestine and windpipe, and its mildly sickening taste of sewers. She likes it when her husband calls her 'my sausage', and considers it a sign of affectionate esteem when others refer to her quite openly as 'Andouillette'.

On the day which concerns us, she and Andouil are setting off on holiday, and our story begins as René Andouil, with his right foot, is playing indolently with the accelerator of his beloved Peugeot. It ticks over contentedly as the dawning sun washes its first pastel shades on to the horizon behind Lisieux, making the sky look like a bathroom whose decor has been chosen by an elderly woman of excellent repute, and René Andouil blinks his eyes and stifles a prolonged yawn with the back of his hand. He loves these early starts to his annual holiday, and does not even resent having to misinform his wife about their projected time of departure. After forty years of marriage, René knows without bitterness that in order to leave at half past six, play loudly on the esplanade until eleven every night, and they turn a mere trip to the supermarket into a veritable nightmare. Every year Andouillette suggests, 'Why don't we get on the ferry at Ouistreham, and go to England?', and every year Andouil agrees, 'Why not?', but every year, nonetheless, they hitch their caravan to the Peugeot, and head off towards the same campsite in the Val de Loire. This is never discussed, because between them they share the same tacit horror of England and the English. 'The food: what a catastrophe. The hooligans: what horror. The language: so ugly, so unpronounceable, so hopeless for true communication. The English: such hypocrites. The hygiene: so primitive. The driving on the left: just asking for accidents. The prices: appalling. The civilisation: how backward. The coffee: brewed for three days and served up with oil on the surface.' Andouil and Andouillette have never been to England, but they know all these things with the absolute certainty of a mathematician who knows without thinking about it that a chair is a chair and that two plus two makes four. No, it is better by far to go to Chisseaux, where they can meet up with Claudine and Pierre. Pierre and René can smoke their pipes and catch small roach in the placid River Cher, whilst Claudine and Andouillette can set up a table directly behind them on the riverbank, play cards and pass comment on the foreign tourists traipsing past on the way to the whimsical chateau of Chenonceaux. The other thing, of course, is that if one travelled across the Channel, one could not take the dog, and tears are apt to spring to the eyes of Andouillette even at the contemplation of the remotest possibility of separation from her beloved Jonnijon.

It is with Jonnijon clutched to her breast that Andouillette emerges from the house for the final time. She settles into the passenger seat, and, turning to her husband, says, 'I wonder, do you think I should go to the toilet one more time?'

'My sausage, you've just been,' replies her husband. 'I heard the noise of the flushing.'

'All the same,' she says. 'You know me and my plumbing.'

It is true. Andouillette's plumbing has been much disarranged by childbirth. Her son began the disarrangement, her daughter compounded it, and a sedentary lifestyle has completed it. Her husband, who enjoys a furtive pleasure in mildly tormenting his wife and playing upon her fears, says, 'Don't worry, we can stop in a little while. I'm sure you can hold on.'

'I'm not so sure,' says his wife, 'am I, Jonnijon?' She ruffles the dog's ears. The dog is the addressee of most of her rhetorical figures. Its stock response is to look interested, lick the air with its tongue, as if bestowing a kiss from a distance, and perform a few token oscillations of its tightly curled backside. 'Jonnijon,' says Andouillette, affectionately kissing its nose. She turns to her husband. 'Don't forget, stop at the first boulangerie that's open, and we'll buy a nice baguette, fresh from the oven.'

'You always say that,' observes Andouil, and he shifts the car into gear. As they depart in the direction of Douvres-la-Délivrande, he says, 'The car is pulling well today,' and Andouillette replies, 'You always say that.'

At about the same time as Andouil and Andouillette are approaching the Caen ring road, the Abbeville chapter of Hell's Angels are leaving town on their substantial black motorcycles to attend the annual French Hell's Angels' convention in Limoges, a town famous for china, a breed of cattle and a particularly fine way of serving magret de canard. Abbeville, on the other hand, is famous for very little, despite its being an enviably pleasant place in which to live. Its small size precludes the existence of a very large chapter of Hell's Angels, which in its heyday in the seventies had consisted of eight young men and ten permanently bewildered young women. One Angel had died in a crash with a combine harvester, one had become a priest, one had moved away and bought a car, and another had joined a heavy metal band, moved on into producing records, and had finished up writing the jingles for television advertisements, his motorcycle rotting under canvas in a barn at his country estate near Angoulême.

The women had all disappeared in the way that women do. The chapter's original intention had been to make of life a perpetual orgy, as Hell's Angels should, and they had adopted the honoured principle that each should have their own woman, whilst there should also be women held in common by the group.

This was how it was done in California, at any rate, but somehow it had never seemed to work out that way in Abbeville. Women theoretically attracted to the macho antics and wild lifestyle of Hell's Angeldom quickly found themselves demoralised by all that swearing, drunkenness, puking, playfighting, fantasising, pennilessness and driving around interminably and pointlessly on motorcycles that always seemed to break down at three o'clock in the morning outside an abattoir in the middle of nowhere. Furthermore, whenever anyone arrived triumphantly with a good bag of drugs with which to get pie-eyed, the substances would turn out to be made of aspirin, or washing powder, or cubed rabbit turds, or trout pellets.

So it is that the Abbeville chapter of Hell's Angels now consists of the four remaining faithful. They themselves work in bakeries or on farms, their children are old enough to find that respectability is the only possible avenue of rebellion, and their wives work for notaries and patisseries. The Angels wear red bandannas to keep the remains of their long grey locks in place. They sport grizzled beards stained with nicotine. They have reflecting sunglasses. They wear grey T-shirts that were white in 1973. They are shod in boots with chrome reinforcements, their legs are cased in black leather trousers, rather uncomfortably tight, and their shoulders are caparisoned in black leather jackets with tasselled sleeves. On their jackets their wives have carefully painted grinning skulls, white daggers dripping with scarlet blood, and various slogans in Gothic script that read 'Death', 'Satan Sucks My Soul' and 'Live Fast, Die Young'. These knights of the road each carry before them an identical pot belly that over-springs the confines of their T-shirts, drooping hirsutely and pendulously over their studded leather belts. Their choppers are old but powerful, painted with diabolical devices, high-decibelled and high-handlebarred. On the road, travelling together at a cool eighty kilometres an hour, our four gallants are still capable of frightening old ladies, outraging the bourgeoisie, and lifting the heart of anyone who has ever succumbed to the romantic dream of the motorcycle and the open road.

We return to Andouillette, whose plumbing, it transpires, is holding up rather better than anticipated. Shortly after passing through Falaise, however, she says to the dog, 'I'm exhausted, aren't I, Jonnijon?' and to her husband, 'These early-morning starts kill me. If I yawn any harder my jaw will break.'

'Put your head back and try and have a sleep,' says Andouil.

'Oh, I can't. I can't sleep sitting up. To sleep I need to lie down.'

'Well, my sausage, you can't lie down.'

'I can lie down in the caravan, can't I?'

Andouil turns and looks at her. He still enjoys the grey light of her eyes and the angular shape of her face. He says, 'If I stop for you to have a sleep, we'll lose all the time we gained by setting out early. We may as well have stayed in bed at home. Really, we want to get to Chisseaux in good time to rendezvous with Pierre and Claudine, and get the caravan stabilised. It's horrible when it's a last-minute rush to beat the darkness.'

'I can sleep in the caravan, and you can keep driving, chéri.'

'Now, come along, my sweet, you know it's illegal. I've told you a hundred times. We have this conversation every time we take the caravan out. God help us if we get caught breaking the law, and anyway, if there's an accident it's very dangerous.' He sees her pouting, and adds, 'I'm only thinking of you, my sausage.'

'I've decided,' says Andouillette. 'I'm going in the caravan, and that's that. I'm tired.'

'You can't,' replies Andouil.

'I'm going to,' she insists.

'When we got married, you promised to obey me,' says Andouil.

'I didn't mean that bit; I only meant the other bits.' Andouillette puts on her 'little-girl-pleading' voice. 'Please, Chouchou. I want to, I want to. I'm a tired little sausage. Please. We've never been stopped, and we've never had an accident. Just this once, just for your little sausage.'

'O, for God's sake,' exclaims Andouil, and he pulls over into a lay-by. Andouillette kisses him gratefully on the cheek, and scurries out to let herself and the dog into the caravan.

Inside, as the car moves off, she struggles to resist the swaying of the vehicle as she undresses and puts on the red satin panties and the extra-brief red satin nightie that Andouil gave her jocularly at Christmas. It was not that Andouil had expected any results from such a gift; their carnal relations had ended more than a decade before, succumbing to a combination of apathy, familiarity, loss of physical confidence and mild diabetes. Nowadays, anyway, Andouillette bestows the best part of her kisses and embraces upon the dog, but she and Andouil still play the formal parts of lovers, and when he gives her a suggestive present she takes it in the spirit of sincere tokenism with which it is intended. Andouillette snuggles down under the duvet and is rocked to sleep as Andouil conducts them in the direction of Argentan, where there is no chapter of Hell's Angels at all.

Past Alençon there is a pleasant patch of woodland at La Feuillère, and it is just there that Andouil, rather than Andouillette, feels stirrings in his plumbing. He has enjoyed a very large bowl of black coffee for breakfast, which he drank for pleasure, plus a small glass of grapefruit juice, which he drank for vague reasons of health. These liquids have been duly processed by the relevant organs, and now reside in their last reservoir, which is sending increasingly urgent telegraphs to the brain of René Andouil. The latter, accordingly, pulls into a deserted lay-by and walks a little way up the road to where there is a small bridge over the ditch, and a pathway into the woods. Andouil relieves himself guiltlessly on to an anthill, and watches the reaction of the ants with some interest. He returns to the Peugeot, and drives on in the direction of Le Mans.

Alas, however, for Andouillette, for she has been awakened by the sudden and unnatural stillness of the caravan, and has realised simultaneously that she too is in need. For a crucial thirty seconds she lies beneath the duvet, calculating, weighing up pros and cons. How much longer will she be able to hold out, if she doesn't go now? Is it worth sacrificing present warmth and somnolence for future comfort? Is it worth getting dressed? Is it worth disturbing Jonnijon, who is also curled up on the bed? Andouillette squeezes the relevant muscles experimentally. She has heard that one can do exercises designed to strengthen them, but she has had a horror of exercise ever since puberty. Finally she decides that she should get up and go, in the spirit of insurance and in the hope of peace. She peeks out of the window and sees that she is in a lay-by, with the door opening straight on to the woods. No need to get dressed, then. She opens the cupboard and takes out the first shoes she finds. They are her husband's, vastly too big, but correspondingly easy to slip on in a hurry. She rummages in a drawer for some lavatory paper. She likes the quilted kind, peach-coloured. She opens the door, glances in both directions to ensure that no one is looking, and creeps up to the passenger side of the car. There is no one in there, so René must be in the woods. She scans the trees for a sign of him, and coos softly, 'Chouchou? Chouchou?' There is no response. By now the prospect of relief has worked its fatal magic, her bladder is on red alert, and she realises that all choice has been taken out of her hands. Reasoning desperately that she will only need a few seconds, she scrambles across the little ditch, and scuttles behind an oak tree with a very substantial trunk.

Accordingly, she and Jonnijon are still engaged in the woods as Andouil and the caravan take off unbeknownst in the direction of Le Mans. Jonnijon is the first to emerge and behold the absence of the caravan; he barks in puzzlement. Andouillette, clad only in her red satin panties and nightie, and a clodhopping pair of her husband's lace-up shoes, puts her hands to her face in horror and runs back into the woods, where she crouches down in the bracken. She listens to the wild thumping of her heart, and clutches Jonnijon to her breast. It is the end of the world, but death is yet too far off. Alone in the woods, in her exiguous red satin and her husband's shoes, equipped only with a roll of lavatory paper, Andouillette begins to cave in and die of mortification. She prays to God and the Virgin for deliverance and salvation. Twigs impress themselves unpleasantly upon her pale flesh, and an ant gets into her shoe and bites her. The bracken smells alien and malevolent. She finds herself too desolate even to weep. She whimpers and keens, and the companionable Jonnijon, anxious not to be left out, begins to howl. The animals of the woods fall silent as they listen in perplexity to the joint despair of woman and dog.

The four Hell's Angels of the Abbeville chapter have passed through Alençon, and are now approaching the woodland of La Feuillère. In the meantime two gendarmes have parked their patrol car out of sight just a couple of kilometres away at La Chesnaie. This is their favourite spot for catching speeding motorists, lorry drivers with bald tyres, motorcycles with defective stoplights, and farmers with overloaded trailers. Concealed by a hedgerow and a farmhouse, they lie in wait as the farmer's wife brings them croissants and coffee. She considers it a good insurance policy, and besides, she is fond of the two young men who, like policemen everywhere, look far too fresh-faced to have the job that they do. She thinks it's rather sweet, the way they put on sunglasses to make themselves look more intimidating. She loves their neatly pressed blue shirts, their neat backsides and their smart kepis. Their holstered pistols give her a pleasant shiver of horror every time that she notices them. She refers to the two gendarmes as 'my boys', and her husband grumbles because they block the access for his tractor. Sergeant Gaspard LaCroix and Officer Michel Mascon are sitting side by side discussing with some ribaldry the possibility of having women serve in the gendarmerie. One of the things they are trained to notice is the absence of a passenger when a car passes that is towing a caravan. It nearly always means that a sleepy woman is in the back, a law has been broken, an offence against the state has been perpetrated. When Andouil passes, alone in the front of his Peugeot, they raise their eyebrows and think of chasing after him. Unanimously and wordlessly, however, they deem it better to finish their coffee whilst it is still hot and their croissants whilst they are still warm. They store Andouil and his caravan in their memories, however, because a gendarme never knows when something observed might turn out to be significant.

The four Hell's Angels are now stopping at a certain lay-by in La Feuillère in order to respond to a call of nature. A cool breeze on the stomach shrinks the bladder, and motorcyclists, even Hell's Angels, have to stop more frequently than four-wheeled motorists. Crouched low in the bracken, her hand clamped firmly around Jonnijon's muzzle, Andouillette feels her heart sink to her feet and rise to her throat simultaneously. She is a respectable bourgeoise, and she has an instinctive ter-ror of anyone on a motorcycle. She has heard four throbbing machines arrive in the lay-by and cut out, she has heard the shuffle of manly feet on the litter of the forest floor, and she has heard rough manly voices laughing gutturally. The four companions are peeing guiltlessly on the same ants' nest sprinkled by Andouil, causing one to speculate as to whether or not in France a special species of ant might have evolved on roadsides and verges, that is resistant to urine, or even capable of turning it to advantage. Andouillette, her heart hammering in her breast, raises her head slowly above the bracken, and sees four apocalyptic apparitions covered in demonic badges and tattoos, their lank hair at shoulder length, their black leather cracked and faded, yet menacing and horrifyingly virile. Andouillette is in the woods, dressed in red satin panties and brief nightie, armed only with a small dog and a roll of lavatory paper, and before her stand four micturating barbarians who are undoubtedly sadists, rapists and murderers. She shrinks back down into the bracken and trembles.

Jonnijon, however, begins to struggle. His ears rise to the crown of his head, and he begins to writhe and twist in Andouillette's arms. His tiny claws rake at her breasts through the red satin, and his brown eyes roll in their sockets. Jonnijon, minuscule though he is, is still a dog, and a dog has to bark when a dog has to bark. All he wants is a chance to do a bit of yelping, and suddenly he scrabbles loose and hurtles out of the bracken in order to bark at the Hell's Angels.

The four friends look down at the dog in some amazement. 'Ooh, look, a poodle,' says one of them.

'What's it doing here?' asks another.

'Must be lost,' says the third.

'Some bastards chuck their animals out of their cars in the middle of nowhere, just to get rid of them,' says the fourth.

'Bastards,' they all murmur together.

'Let's look at the tattoo on the inside of its ear,' suggests the first, 'then we can take it to the police and let them deal with it.'

'If we can catch the little fucker,' says the second.

'I wish it would stop barking,' says the third, 'it's driving me crazy.'

'I'll throw my jacket on it,' says the fourth, 'and that way we can grab it without being bitten. These little dogs have the worst bites. I heard of a postman who had to have his leg amputated.'

He removes his leather jacket and advances upon Jonnijon like a matador with his cape. Jonnijon knows that he is being hunted and backs away, yelping furiously. He is bouncing up and down as if on springs, and is reversing relentlessly in the direction of Andouillette.

Andouillette has not heard the conversation properly, but through the fronds she can see the Hell's Angel advancing on her beloved Jonnijon. Andouillette has visions of Jonnijon being eaten, tortured to death, or sacrificed to the devil, and suddenly her maternal instincts surge like a tidal wave out of whatever organ it is wherein they dwell, and invade every molecule of her being. Where there was terror and panic, there is now invincible courage and warlike ferocity. She has become the Jeanne d'Arc of the Forest of La Feuillère. She springs suddenly out of her place of concealment with a wild and unearthly shriek, and the four Hell's Angels and Jonnijon cry out and flee together into the shelter of the trees. Hell's Angel Number One trips over a tree root and falls. Number Two tumbles into the ditch at the side of the road. Number Three is arrested in mid-flight by a bramble that catches in his beard and rakes fine bloody lines across his face. Number Four makes it back to the bikes, and begins senselessly to try to flag down the traffic.

The pale faces of drivers and passengers regard him with the kind of intrigued interest that zoo visitors reserve for a gorilla that is playing marbles with its own faeces.

It is some time before order is restored. The four Angels, who have so often talked of raising the devil or some few of his demons, have been confronted by the genuine article, and have been undone by horripilation. They have seen a squat creature in costume as scarlet as the flames of hell, with fat, pallid, mottled legs, a halo of coarse and chaotic bluish hair framing a white face streaked with black, baring its crooked yellow teeth. The demon has blood-red fingernails and lips. It has leaped out at them, whooping fearsomely, and within a fraction of a second they have all reverted to the naive Catholicism of their youth. They cross themselves and beg the Virgin for protection, peeking out from under the bracken and behind the trees. Jonnijon regards his mistress from the safety of a foxhole, and decides to come out later. He yaps pointlessly.

Inevitably our four intrepid heroes come slowly to the realisation that they have in fact been confronted by a lady in late middle age, in much distress, clad somewhat saucily, it is true, but who is interested only in rescuing her dog. Hell's Angel Number One rises to his feet and faces her to be joined slowly and shamefacedly by his companions. Hell's Angel Number Two points to her feet and says wonderingly, 'You've got men's shoes on.'

Andouillette waves her roll of lavatory paper at them. 'Don't you dare touch me. If you so much as move a little finger to touch me, I'll do such things … such things … such things as you wouldn't believe …'

The Hell's Angels look at each other. It is true that they have spent half of their lifetimes thinking and talking about being bad – it is a philosophy, after all, about the intensification of experience by means of extremes – but it is also true that none of them has ever succeeded in behaving very badly.

'Do you think she's mad?' asks Number Four.

'Could be,' says Number Two, 'she's got men's shoes on.'

'They are my husband's,' says Andouillette with dignity. 'I have been left here accidentally.'

A mere ten minutes later, after explanations have been made and tranquillity re-established, we find Andouillette riding pillion behind Hell's Angel Number One. She is feeling very chilly, so she is holding tightly on to him with her arms around his generous embonpoint. In between them is Jonnijon, squeezed between his back and her breasts, peering forwards over the satanic Angel's right shoulder. Jonnijon blinks against the slipstream, and his tightly curled ears float behind him. He is too befuddled to panic or to bark. He watches the world go by at incomprehensible speed, and feels a little nauseous.

Our knights of the road have agreed to help Andouillette find her husband and her caravan, and they are transporting her in great style along the N138 in the direction of Le Mans. Those on the roadside stop and gawp, and those drivers coming in the other direction perform classic double takes. As the eccentric convoy passes La Feuillère and the concealment of the two gendarmes, two croissants stop halfway to two mouths, and two small cups of coffee are tipped quickly down two throats. Sergeant Gaspard LaCroix guns the patrol car into life and pulls out in the wake of the Angels, his siren ululating and his blue light flashing. Officer Michel Mascon reports in on the radio that they are pursuing some vehicles behaving suspiciously, and within sixty seconds they are overtaking the Angels and waving them into the side of the road. The collective heart of the Hell's Angels sinks. They are always being picked on by the police. They have learned to switch off their engines promptly and be very polite. They used to talk eagerly about beating up policemen, but the only time they had a chance, they ended up giving them cigarettes and talking about motorbikes.

The gendarmes adjust their sunglasses on the bridges of their noses and walk with studied coolness back to where the Angels await them. Officer Mascon puts his hand briefly on to the flap of his holster, as if to imply something, and Sergeant Gaspard LaCroix approaches Hell's Angel Number One. 'Driving licence,' he says. The licence is produced. 'Identity card,' says the sergeant. All the cards are collected, except for that of Andouillette, who has been studiously ignored, as if the officers cannot resist saving the greatest challenge and the greatest mystery until last.

Sergeant LaCroix speaks whilst Officer Mascon stands next to him with his arms folded. He addresses Angel Number One. 'You are François LeBreton?'

'Yes, sir.'

'On your driving licence and on your identity card you have put a line through your name, and written "Abaddon".'

'It's my *nom de diable*,' explains François LeBreton. 'Abaddon is the destroying Angel of the Apocalypse.'

'I see,' says the sergeant. He turns to Angel Number Two. 'And you are Robert Derives, alias "Donachiel"?'

'It's an angel you invoke to command demons,' explains Robert.

'I see,' repeats the sergeant, and to Angel Number Three he says, 'And you are Jerome Laforge, alias "Arioch"?'

'Angel of vengeance,' says Jerome. 'It means "Fierce Lion".'

'I see,' reiterates the sergeant, and to Angel Number Four he says, 'And you are Antoine Dupont, alias "Mammon"?'

'Yes, sir. Mammon is the Prince of Avarice, Prince of Tempters, and Hell's Ambassador to England.'

'I've been to England,' interpolates Officer Michel Mascon, 'and it was Hell. I don't see why Hell should want to send an ambassador to itself.'

'That's a good point,' says the sergeant, and Antoine says, 'I've been thinking of changing my name to "Marchosias".

'You gentleman,' pronounces Sergeant LaCroix, 'are all guilty of defacing documents belonging to the state. You might all be charged for this offence.'

Angel Number One speaks up: 'It's the kind of pen that you can rub out with an eraser. It's not a proper defacement.'

'Are you telling me when a defacement is or is not a deface-ment?' demands the sergeant.

'It is an interesting question, Sergeant,' observes Officer Mascon. 'It probably isn't a simple issue.'

'Thank you, Officer. Are you also aware that in not wearing the requisite protective headgear, you are committing an add-itional offence?'

'We are wearing these,' says Antoine with great humility, 'they're quite strong.'

'A black leather Stetson, with silver skulls and crossbones and enamelled confederate flags does not qualify as a crash helmet.'

'Angels don't wear crash helmets,' says Jerome.

'Why don't you get black ones and paint skulls on them?' suggests Officer Mascon.

'I suppose we could,' agrees Robert Derives, 'it would seem like a decent compromise.'

'In my career I have scraped a great many motorcyclists' brains from the tarmac,' announces Sergeant Gaspard LaCroix sententiously, and then he turns to Andouillette, who has witnessed all this with an apathy born of having already experienced too much in one short day. 'As for you, madame, you too are inappropriately dressed for motorcycling. I might even suggest that there is an element of indecency. Identity card, please. Incidentally, my colleague and I have been wondering whether you might be in need of any assistance. Our initial impression was that you may be with these gentlemen against your will.'

'It's in the caravan,' said Andouillette, 'my identity card, that is. And I'm not being kidnapped. We're just trying to catch my husband.'

'What about the dog?' demands Officer Michel Mascon. 'Isn't it an offence to carry livestock insecurely on a motorcycle?'

'We'll have to look that one up,' says the sergeant, and Andouillette exclaims, 'He's not livestock, he's Jonnijon.'

'What's this about a caravan?' asks the sergeant, his mind tweaked by a recent memory.

So it was that ten minutes later a gendarmerie patrol car containing two gendarmes and Andouillette sets off in the direction of Le Mans, followed by a small escort of Hell's Angels, all of them intent upon playing a little joke upon the hapless Andouil, who is duly flagged down by Officer Mascon just past St-Jean-d'Asse. He finds himself facing two very young gendarmes, and a circle of grinning Hell's Angels in early middle age. One of them has fine lines of congealed blood upon his face.

Andouil is the kind of man who, in any situation in which he feels anxiety, begins to pour with sweat. On this occasion he begins to sweat immediately, and his anxiety about sweating so much causes him to sweat even more profusely. He mops his brow with his handkerchief, and within moments it is sodden. He begins to feel anxious about not having another handkerchief. The perspiration cascades off his face on to his lap. The gendarmes smile to each other confidingly. This is the telltale reaction of a thoroughly guilty man.

'Good afternoon, sir,' says Sergeant LaCroix coolly, adjusting his sunglasses and leaning down to the window. 'Driving licence? Identity card?'

Officer Mascon leans over and says, 'You wouldn't be called Behemoth, or Beelzebub, or anything like that?' and Andouil shakes his head miserably.

'Going on holiday are you, sir?' asks LaCroix, and Andouil nods. The muscles of his neck feel slightly out of control.

'On your own? That's not very jolly, is it?'

'I'm meeting my wife at Chisseaux. It's near Chenonceaux.'

'You wouldn't have anyone in the caravan, then?'

'Oh no, Officer. It's illegal.'

'He knows the law,' says LaCroix to Mascon. 'It's so heartening when civilians know the law. Makes our job so much easier.' Turning back to Andouil, he says, 'So you wouldn't mind if we take a look in the back?'

Andouil's heart thuds, and perspiration continues to pour off him. He looks from the gendarmes to the Hell's Angels and back again. There is something appallingly ominous about the way in which they are nudging each other and exchanging

hopes that he can identify the place where he stopped to pee. He shivers in advance at what Andouillette will say and do to him. The prospect is so terrifying that he even considers abandoning her altogether. Suddenly Andouillette steps out from behind the caravan and confronts him. She is dressed like a harlot, her hair is frighteningly dishevelled, her maquillage has been smeared into an expressionist nightmare, she is clutching Jonnijon and a roll of lavatory paper, and she is wearing a ludicrously disproportionate and anomalous pair of men's lace-up shoes, that, a moment later, he identifies as his own.

She throws herself into his arms with a stifled little cry, and he finds Jonnijon crushed against his chest. Andouillette steps back, puts the dog on the ground carefully, squares herself, and slaps Andouil resoundingly across the face. His bifocals reorganise themselves so that the left lens settles on the tip of his nose. Uttering one obscenity so vile that it has never escaped her lips in her life before, she shoves him violently in the chest. He sits down on the ground in wonderment, and feels a stinging bruise grow like a mushroom on his cheek.

That night in the safety of the campsite in Chisseaux, Andouil and Andouillette lie in bed and cuddle each other so tightly that it is almost like making love. He has the imprint of her palm turning to shades of green and lilac on his left cheek. In his basket under the table Jonnijon squeaks as he dreams about the most confusing day of his life. His eyes are itching because of the ride, and his ribs ache from having been so often and so violently clutched to his mistress's chest.

Andouil is half asleep, he is blushing and perspiring because he has been reliving the humiliation of driving away and finding the gendarmes and the Hell's Angels waiting one kilometre down the road, all in a posse, waving and smirking as he passes them in the direction of Le Mans. He is sure that they can see the bruise growing on his cheek.

Andouillette stirs and says, 'Chéri?'

Andouil wakes a little, and murmurs, 'Yes, my sausage?'

'I've had an idea. You mightn't like it, though.'

'Well, what is it? There's no harm in asking.'

Andouillette pauses. Her silence becomes ominous. Andouil is almost relieved when at last she says, 'Do you think we're too old to have a motorbike?'

'We could have a sidecar with a lavatory in it,' says Andouil.

A DAY OUT FOR MEHMET ERBIL

Mehmet Erbil slung his tattered but faithful white plastic sack over his shoulder and stepped off the ferry at Kilitbahir. It was a short and easy crossing from Çanakkale, and he always enjoyed it. He would contemplate the choppy waves, keep an eye open for good-looking girls, and take in the spectacle of Sultan Mehmet II's castle as it grew nearer and more distinct. It always made him think of harder and wilder times in centuries past, when sultans took titles such as 'Shedder of Blood', 'The Grim' or 'The Merciless', and mighty cannon roared across the Dardanelles to deter impudent Russians, pirates and invaders. The only trouble with the crossing was that it took up money, eating into his tiny profits, and increasing the despair that gnawed away at his hope. 'One day I will have money,' he thought. 'One day I won't have to live like a dog. One day I won't have to do this work. Or perhaps it will always be like this; perhaps I will die as I have lived, in hardship and ignominy.' Mehmet's sole concern was that, in the conduct of his daily life, he should earn just slightly more than he was obliged to spend. It was a question not merely of survival, but of personal pride.

Mehmet evidenced his pride by taking care of his appearance. His light blue trousers were carefully pressed; his shoes, worn down at the heel and scuffed though they might be, were thoroughly polished. His shirt was clean, and the collar had been removed and then sewn back on the other way so that the frayed side was invisible. His woollen waistcoat was neatly darned in wool that was almost of the same hue as the original, and the brass buckle of his belt was well rubbed to bring out its shine. He carried his shoulders well back and square, as he had learned during the years of his national service, and his black hair was clean, neatly trimmed and lightly greased into place. One would not have known that Mehmet Erbil was desperate, unless one looked into his pained and evasive dark brown eyes and noted how he smoked successive cigarettes with the air of someone who compulsively resorts to remedies that time and experience have proven to be inefficacious. Mehmet also smelled faintly of beer, which was the one medicine for world-weariness that he could actually afford. He was forty-one years old, he was thin but reasonably fit, and his skin was darker than most on account of his wanderings with the white sack. His other career had imbued him with the habit of glancing frequently at his cheap but functional black plastic watch.

It was May 19th, and Mehmet was taking full advantage of National Youth and Sports Day. He had gone dutifully to his local school and had stood in the sun, since the canny women had got to the shaded places earlier than the men, and had watched the youngsters being put through their paces. When he was young he had been a good runner, and it filled him with wistfulness to see the boys, their arms pumping as they sped around the track. It was more amusing to watch the girls' races, because you could tell that their hearts were not in it. He cheered ironically, along with all the others, when, in the five hundred metres, two of the girls ran out of breath with one hundred metres to go, and peeled off sheepishly, to disappear into the crowd.

Mehmet listened to the numerous speeches, in which there was not one sentence that did not somehow manage to mention Mustafa Kemal, and he stood through the formation manoeuvres. About a hundred boys in white shirts and black trousers did a kind of choric callisthenic display of such length that he marvelled at their memory rather than their prowess, and then the girls did something equally long and elaborate, each of them clutching a huge red fan, boldly emblazoned with the white crescent moon and star. The best display by far was performed by a small group of girls in scarlet robes, their foreheads adorned with gold coins, who gracefully danced, clutching large silver trays in their hands, stepping and swaying together to a long and ululating melody rendered by a small band that consisted of clarinet, violin and drum. Having done his duty to the school and to National Youth and Sports Day, Mehmet slipped away, and took the ferry across to Kilitbahir.

Mehmet had been correct in supposing that patriotic coachloads of school parties would be converging on the sites and monuments of the Gallipoli peninsula, and it was with satisfaction that he noted the swarms of teenagers clambering over the remains of the gun batteries, prodding the wild tortoises, posing on the battlements of the castle, and scattering Coca-Cola cans in the wake of their thirst. It was only May 19th, and the onset of summer's implacable heat was yet a few days off, but it was hot enough nonetheless for the schoolchildren to be buying plenty of soft drinks. Mehmet set about his work.

At about midday he felt there was not much more to be done for the time being, and he decided that he would try to cadge a lift to the great monument at Mount Hisarlik Tepe. Accordingly he set off along the sinuous coastal road, in the secure knowledge that before long someone would give him a lift. In a country where most people had no car, but everyone could still be trusted, it was accepted that one gave lifts as a matter of course. Before long, a white car passed him and he signalled frantically for it to stop. When it did, he picked up his white sack and sprinted.

When he arrived at the passenger door, he bent down to look at the driver, and knew immediately that he had flagged down a foreigner. The fellow was wearing shorts, white socks and a straw hat. His face, forearms and legs were burned a painful brick red by the sun, and he had the strength and bulk of someone who had flourished in a land of plenty. Like many foreigners, he looked somewhat ridiculous, and Mehmet wondered whether he would be safe to drive with. Also, foreigners were usually quite rich, and this often seemed to bring with it some unpleasant and offensive attitudes.

'*Günaydin*,' said the foreigner, and Mehmet thought, 'At least he speaks Turkish.'

The driver was in fact a phrasebook foreigner. He had conscientiously learned all the phrases he needed to know for telling people that he did not understand and did not speak Turkish. He had been hoping that in this way he might avoid the embarrassment of having to listen intelligently and nod at appropriate moments whenever Turks engaged him in conversation. He had discovered, however, that Turks were like the English: they thought that if they talked loudly enough in their own language, and paraphrased and reparaphrased themselves often enough, then sooner or later a foreigner would grasp their point. This particular foreigner had also come up against the usual difficulty of the phrasebook user: it was all very well being able to ask things in Turkish, but one never understood what one's interlocutor said in reply. He asked '*Nerede?*', and immediately knew that he was not going to comprehend Mehmet's response.

'Well,' said Mehmet, 'I'm just going round and about, sort of following all of these school parties, so I'm not really fussy. If you're going by any of the monuments, perhaps you could just drop me off.'

The foreigner looked at him blankly, and said, '*Anlamam. Turkçe bilmiyorum.*'

Mehmet furrowed his brow and looked at him through the window. 'Well, that's very odd, that you tell me in Turkish that you don't understand Turkish and you don't speak it. You must admit it's a little peculiar.'

The foreigner shrugged and raised his hands in a gesture of helplessness. '*Anlamam,*' he repeated, and again asked, '*Nerede?*'

'I've already told you where I'm going,' said Mehmet. He was beginning to wonder whether the foreigner might not be a little mad, and whether it might not be better to wait for another car. He waved his hand in the direction of Seddülbahir. 'Look,' he said, 'there's only one road and only one direction, so that's where I'm going.'

'*Anlamam. Turkçe bilmiyorum,*' repeated the foreigner, with the same dumb expression upon his face. Mehmet sighed, realising that he had let himself in for a difficult lift, but he opened the door anyway, dumped his plastic sack on the floor, and climbed in. If he was going to get this foreigner to understand anything, then he was going to have to repeat himself an awful lot.

'No problem,' said the foreigner, and Mehmet's eyes lit up. This was universal language. 'No problem,' he repeated, nodding his head as the car pulled away.

On their left the Marmara Sea glowed in the sun, lapping on the tiny beaches, and above them on their right rose the slopes of dense Mediterranean scrub. Mehmet began to relax; the foreigner might be strange, but he was a careful driver. He reached into his shirt pocket and extracted a crushed pack of cigarettes. He had already lit one when he remembered that some of the more outlandish foreigners go crazy if you smoke anywhere near them. He indicated the cigarette and raised anxious eyebrows. 'OK?' he asked.

'No problem,' said the foreigner, and Mehmet repeated the phrase happily. He offered his packet of cigarettes to the driver, who indicated 'no' by a small wave of his hand. Mehmet considerately held his cigarette out of the window so that its smoke would not offend. The foreigner noticed, and, having once been a smoker, became anxious that in the slipstream the cigarette would burn out too quickly. He pulled out the ashtray in the dashboard, and gestured towards it. 'OK, no problem,' he said.

Mehmet smiled. He too had been anxious about the cigarette being largely wasted. 'I suppose you're a tourist,' observed Mehmet. 'I suppose you're going around taking photos of everything. We get a lot of tourists here. Australians, New Zealanders, Germans. Where do you come from?'

'*Evet*,' replied the foreigner, who was tired of saying 'I don't understand. I don't speak Turkish' and thought that he might be able to get away with simply saying, 'Yes.' Mehmet looked at him askance; the foreigner's brain must be a little disconnected. They passed an old peasant woman whose donkey was laden with firewood. 'Fotograf?' he suggested, assuming that the foreigner would like to take snaps of the peninsula's more picturesque sights. He felt mildly insulted when the foreigner shook his head. 'Well, I suppose you just want to take pictures of the monuments,' said Mehmet. 'Perhaps your grandfather is buried in one of the cemeteries.'

The foreigner thought it safe to continue to reply in the affirmative, even though he did not understand at all. '*Evet,*' he said, unwittingly assenting to the proposition that his grandfather lay thereabouts in a hero's grave.

'Well,' said Mehmet, 'my grandfather fought in that campaign as well. Obviously it was on the Turkish side. You should have heard his stories. They were amazing. He got shot three times on the same day, and then he was bitten by a snake. He lived through all that, and the war of national liberation (the one against the Greeks), and then he lived until he was ninety-seven years old.' Mehmet grew serious. 'You know, it's true what Atatürk said, that the war we fought made us respect each other. The effect of all that blood was to make us brothers. English, Anzac, French, Turkish, all brothers.' He looked very intently into the foreigner's face, and asked, 'Don't you agree?'

The foreigner resorted once again to '*Anlamam. Turkçe bilmiyorum*', and Mehmet shook his head. This foreigner was undoubtedly a bit strange, agreeing with you part of the time, and then saying that he doesn't understand. Perhaps there was some interesting psychological or intellectual condition whereby you momentarily forget your foreign languages, and then remembered them again a few minutes later.

Mehmet made the foreigner drive to the huge monument and war cemetery at Hisarlik Tepe. It was forty-two metres high and was visible for miles around. Mehmet naturally assumed that the foreigner would want to photograph it, as well as all the heroic statues that surrounded it, and he elected himself to be the guide. In fact, it was really a stroke of luck that he had been given a lift by a tourist, since this would take him to all the sites where the parties of schoolchildren were.

Mehmet left his white sack in the car, and the foreigner reluctantly took pictures of the monument, and the cemetery, and of Mehmet smiling in front of the statues. He had come to Turkey with only a limited amount of film, and did not know how to explain to Mehmet that he was a botanist who was visiting the peninsula to study the wildflowers, which at this time of year bloomed prolifically in all the fields and grassy banks. The Turkish farmers did not use herbicides, and the wheat fields were swathed in scarlet poppies. The botanist found it depressing to think that once upon a time his own country had been as lovely as this, and he also found it frustrating that he was unable to explain to Mehmet that he was interested not in Turkey's valiant past, but in its flowers. All the same, he was moved when he saw the tears in the corners of Mehmet's eyes as he read the names of the soldiers on the gravestones. Two beautiful teenage girls were walking together, arm in arm, reverently placing bunches of marguerites on the graves. He found himself wishing that he was able to love his own country as much as the Turks loved theirs.

Mehmet picked up an abandoned Coca-Cola can, and the botanist thought, 'Ah, what a good man, he cares enough about this place to pick up other people's rubbish.' The botanist was very strong on the idea that each of us is responsible for the environment. In his own country he had often got into trouble with groups of youths, on account of confronting them and demanding that they pick up their sweet papers and cigarette packets. Mehmet crushed the tin can in his hands, and held on to it. The botanist was surprised that he did not put it in the bins that they passed. He was even more surprised when Mehmet signalled him to continue walking, and then rummaged in one of the bins.

Mehmet was ashamed of having been reduced to this, and he did not want the foreigner to see what he was doing. The foreigner, however, was perplexed; his immediate thought was that Mehmet must be an oddity, perhaps someone who was obsessed with rubbish. However, he saw Mehmet's hurried shame very clearly, and pretended, when Mehmet caught him up, not to notice that he was carrying three or four cans behind his back. The foreigner let Mehmet back into the car, and affected not to notice that he was hurriedly stuffing them into his white sack.

The foreigner spotted a can on his side of the car, thought about it, picked it up, and, when he got in, handed it to his passenger. Mehmet looked up at him, took the can eagerly, and then felt the blood rush to his face and ears. His expression became miserable; he had been detected so soon in his humiliating occupation. He tried to explain.

'I do it for money,' he said. 'I've got a proper job, but it's the inflation. They say it's ninety per cent, but I think it's more like three hundred. Everything's getting more and more expensive, and life is harder and harder every day. I can't afford anything any more. The prices go up and up, and my salary doesn't.' He reached into his back pocket and drew out his wallet. He showed the foreigner his small wad of lira. 'Turkish lira,' he said disgustedly, 'they're not worth anything. I don't know whose fault it is, but they ought to be shot. How am I supposed to manage? Unlike some, I've got nobody sending me Deutschmarks. It's a shitty life.'

The foreigner nodded; he needed no Turkish to understand the gist of these gestures and complaints; there were so many zeros on a Turkish banknote that even a dog was a multimillionaire.

Mehmet reached into his sack and showed the foreigner the bottom of a tin can. 'I look at the serial numbers,' he said, 'and that way I know which ones I ought to collect. Some are made of good metal that's worth recycling, and some of them aren't. I only take the best.'

The foreigner thought for a moment. He had two days left, which was probably enough time for the fieldwork that he had to do. It looked as though he would just have to give up the idea of spending the last day lounging on a beach. It was frustrating that Mehmet had somehow taken over his day, but on the other hand he was in a splendid position to help him, since he had the car and plenty of time. He criticised himself inwardly for being tempted to let Mehmet wander off somewhere, and then speed away in the car. He would have despised himself for doing it, and besides, how often does one get the chance to help someone else earn an honest living? He felt obscurely that his comfortable life on a comfortable income placed a special obligation upon him, and anyway, a few hours collecting cans was surely pleasant enough on a day as lovely and springlike as this. 'Seddülbahir?' he suggested, and Mehmet nodded. There would be lots of schoolchildren at the First Martyrs' Memorial and at the Sergeant Yahya Memorial, all swigging soft drinks and throwing away the cans.

As they drove around the coast the foreigner marvelled all over again that this idyllic place had been the scene of so many months of bloody battles. Mehmet waved a hand towards the fields and their swathes of flowers. 'I love this place,' he said. 'I used to know it very intimately. I did my degree in agronomy, at the university in Istanbul, and I came out here to do my fieldwork. I know the names and habitats of all these flowers, but unfortunately no one in the real world is interested in such things. Nobody pays you for it, anyway. I'm like most of my friends: I've got qualifications I can't use, and I scrape through life like a stray dog in the street. If you've got the time I'd like to go for a short stroll and have a look at the flowers, for old times' sake. Some of them are very interesting. I was working on the use of selective herbicides to get rid of them, but you can't get peasants to spend money on herbicides anyway, and now I'm quite glad that nothing came of my work.' He turned and looked at the stranger. 'I like the flowers now, even though they used to be the enemy.'

'*Anlamam*,' said the foreign botanist hopelessly, frustrated and irritated that Mehmet kept on talking without seeming to realise that no communication was occurring.

Mehmet was also wearied by the lack of communication, however. 'Oh well,' he said, 'I suppose we'll just have to go on looking at these monuments. I don't really see the attraction of it myself, but there you are. At least there'll be a lot of kids throwing away cans.'

At the Cape Helles monument Mehmet became excited by the thought that perhaps the dead grandfather of the stranger was mentioned on the walls or the obelisk, but the latter did not seem to want to go and look. In fact, he had already set about picking up tin cans. Mehmet approached the owner of the refreshments stall, stood with as much dignity as he could, and said to its proprietor, 'I am recycling cans as a sideline, and I am wondering if you might give me your permission to sift through your rubbish bins. I will leave no mess, I promise.'

The proprietor considered him, and nodded his head with resignation. It was hard to have to maintain oneself in any profession these days. 'Who's the foreigner?' he asked.

'I've no idea,' said Mehmet. 'He's a mystery. He picked me up when I was hitching, and now he's just driving me about whilst I pick up cans. I don't know what he's up to or where he's really going.'

'Not all foreigners are shits,' observed the proprietor, a middle-aged man with a comfortable paunch. 'Maybe you've struck it lucky.'

'All the same,' said Mehmet, 'it's a bit strange, driving me about and collecting cans when he doesn't have to.'

'Don't question God's plans,' said the proprietor, pleased with his little flash of pious wisdom, 'maybe he's your angel for the day.'

'That's a pretty thought,' said Mehmet, and the stallholder nodded knowingly, saying, 'God's the boss.'

'Perhaps you could lend me a plastic bag?' suggested Mehmet. 'My sack is getting heavy.'

Mehmet rifled through the rubbish bins, and then he and the foreigner trailed in the wake of the schoolchildren, who were photographing each other in the gun emplacements, and by the Sergeant Yahya Memorial. The foreigner was a little disappointed when he saw that Mehmet was simply discarding cans that he did not deem to be worth recycling; he had still not quite disabused himself of his first faulty notion that Mehmet was an environmentalist. 'All the same,' he thought, 'this fellow is certainly a good rather than a bad thing. At least half of the cans get collected that wouldn't otherwise.'

Mehmet had not eaten since breakfast, and had not really eaten properly for several days. His stomach was starting to rumble, and he was feeling somewhat weak and dizzy. It was by now late afternoon, the heat of the late spring was beginning to oppress the brain, and he was longing for a beer. The trouble was, that if he invited the stranger to a *pastahane*, then it would be up to him to pay for the drinks and a snack. The thought made him panic a little; he was a generous and honourable man, but money was the one thing with which he could not possibly afford to be generous. Nonetheless, he asked, 'Hungry?' in a tentative and non-committal tone of voice.

The word '*acikmak*' was one that the foreigner knew from his phrasebook, and he shook his head. He had been trying to lose weight, and had deliberately been missing out lunch, which in general was quite easy to do when you were tramping about in the wilderness, looking for flowers. Additionally, the equable climate made him feel less greedy than usual, and it was actually quite nice just to drink a litre of water at midday. He was puzzled by Mehmet's response to his denial of hunger, however; he seemed both relieved and disappointed. It occurred to him that perhaps the Turk was angling for a free meal, and this thought at once annoyed him and made him feel sorry.

Mehmet glanced at his watch, and realised that before long he would have to return to the ferry port in order to catch the boat, reluctant as he was to leave behind so many collectible cans, and therefore he suggested, 'Kilitbahir?'

'OK,' said the foreigner, both amused and bemused by the manner in which he had lost a complete day going in a big circle with a perfect stranger.

On the way through the dense pine forest that had been the site of the second battle of Krithia, they both simultaneously spotted a heap of rubbish that had been jettisoned by the roadside. They exchanged glances, and the foreigner stopped the car and reversed. 'At least we now understand each other a little,' they both thought. They found seven cans. 'Seven,' said Mehmet, pleased, and '*yedi*' repeated the foreigner, also pleased.

The foreign botanist stopped the car at an open-air café on the side of the road by the Havuzlar cemetery, intending to buy Mehmet food and drink, but was beaten to it by Mehmet, who ordered a beer for himself and an orange juice for the driver. 'Would you permit me to take away your used tin cans?' Mehmet asked the patron. 'I recycle them, you see. It's a little extra money for the family. I promise I won't make a mess.'

The patron weighed this proposition and gave his assent with a shrug; everyone had to struggle and improvise these days. The government changes, and the problems stay the same.

'Who's the foreigner?' he asked, puzzled that a tin collector should be chauffeured about in a nice new car.

'I don't know who he is,' said Mehmet. 'He's been driving me around all day, helping me collect cans. Someone suggested earlier that he might be my angel.' Mehmet giggled. 'Anyway, I don't know anything about him except that he speaks Turkish, but doesn't understand when I speak it back. It's very strange.'

'Maybe he's deaf,' proposed the patron.

'No, I'm sure he's not,' replied Mehmet. 'But anyway, we've collected hundreds of cans today.'

'I'll tell you what,' said the patron, 'since he's been so good to a Turk, I'm not going to charge you for his drink, OK? I'll give you some of your money back.'

'You're a saint,' exclaimed Mehmet. 'May the blessings of God be upon you.'

'It's nothing,' shrugged the patron. 'If a foreigner can be kind to you, then I can too.'

Later, back at Kilitbahir, Mehmet found that he still had twenty minutes to collect cans before the ferry departed, and that renewed coachloads of patriotic schoolchildren had liberally strewn the grounds of the old castle with drinks cans. He became quite agitated about this bonus, and his natural generosity got the better of him. At the café he ordered a cheese-toast for the stranger, as if he could assuage his own hunger by offering food to another. The waiter was somewhat reluctant to take a food order, since the kitchens were not yet opened, but Mehmet waxed eloquent about the duty of hospitality to foreigners, and stated firmly that the stranger had not eaten for ages. The waiter eyed the plump foreigner sceptically, but ultimately could not refuse this appeal to his honour. He went and got the cheese-toast ready.

Mehmet signalled to the stranger that he was going to go and look for cans whilst they waited for the food. He was thinking that it would be so painful to watch the other eating when he was so hungry himself that it would be better to be out and about. Accordingly he stayed away from the restaurant as long as he possibly could.

The foreigner began to be uneasy and suspicious about Mehmet's long absence. What if he had gone back to the car? His passport was in there. Where the hell was Mehmet?

carefully into his shirt pocket, and then eagerly knocked back the beer that had been waiting for him. When they got up to go, he very deliberately left the can on the table.

He was vexed and consternated to discover that the foreigner had already paid the bill, his vexation being exacerbated by the realisation that he was also quite relieved. He turned angrily on the stranger, but was completely disarmed by the big smile on the latter's face. Mehmet threw up his arm in mock exasperation. 'You are a very bad man,' he said, 'you tricked me.'

Mehmet enquired of the waiter as to whether any of the staff spoke the foreigner's language, and was pleased to discover that there was one. For a short while he talked to the waiter, who then approached the foreigner: 'Mr Mehmet says that he likes you very much, and he wants to know if you like him very much, because you have spent the whole day with him.'

The foreigner was slightly embarrassed. 'Tell him that he is a very good man, and that I like him very much.' He put his hand on his friend's upper arm, and patted it in a brotherly manner.

When Mehmet heard this translated, he found it hard to dominate his emotions. He embraced the foreigner, squeezing his shoulders in his surprisingly strong hands, and looking away so that no one would notice the sentimental tears that were threatening to well up in his eyes. Apart from a decent living, all that Mehmet Erbil really wanted in life was a little honest respect, and it was not often that he received any.

The foreigner presented Mehmet with a business card, upon which he had added his country's code. He knew that if Mehmet telephoned, they would not understand each other one little bit, but it was the gesture that mattered, after all.

Mehmet found a scrap of paper in his wallet, and wrote his own address and telephone number. As an afterthought, he added his profession: '*oğretmen*'.

Mehmet walked with the foreigner back to the car, and for a moment the latter wondered whether Mehmet was thinking of coming to Eçeabat; but Mehmet just wanted to see the foreigner off. He shook his hand repeatedly, saying, 'It would be nice if you came over with your car to Çanakkale. You've got my address. It would be wonderful to see you. It's a shame to go back whilst there's still light,' he grinned, 'and plenty of cans to collect, but I've got four classes tomorrow. I've got to prepare the lessons for the kids, you know how it is, and I've got a mountain of exercise books to mark. What a job, what a life.'

The foreigner was as nonplussed by this speech as he had been by all of Mehmet's remarks. He had given up saying '*Anlamam*' and '*Turkçe bilmiyorum*' and had even given up saying '*Evet*'. Mehmet talked anyway. He saw the foreigner's perplexity, and continued, 'I suppose you're wondering why I came over on the ferry to collect cans when I could have collected them at home in Çanakkale.' Mehmet scratched the back of his neck, and then stroked his chin. 'Well, I wouldn't want any of my own pupils to see me doing this.' He raised the bulging white sack. 'It's not just a question of my self-esteem. No, it's not that. It's that I want my pupils to value education. I want them growing up to think that a schoolteacher is a fine thing to be. It would not be good for them to know that we are reduced to collecting cans.'

The foreigner did not understand, but he knew that Mehmet had been speaking of grave matters. He nodded, and Mehmet nodded too, glad that something had been cleared up.

Mehmet and the foreigner kissed on both cheeks. In the foreigner's country men never did this, but here in Turkey it seemed completely natural and unremarkable, although the scrape of another man's stubble on his cheek did feel distinctly novel and disconcerting.

With a clatter, Mehmet hoisted the white sack on to his shoulder and began to walk away. Over his shoulder he called, 'Remain well.'

'*Güle güle*,' returned the foreigner, remembering the correct formula from his phrasebook. He got into the car and drove away without looking back, knowing that Mehmet would not eat the cheese-toast until he was out of sight, and wanting to give him the chance to eat it as soon as he could.

Back at the hotel the foreigner transferred Mehmet's details to his address book, and then looked up '*oğretmen*' in his Turkish dictionary. He was deeply puzzled to find that it meant 'schoolmaster', and it dawned on him only very slowly that Mehmet must already have had a proper job, and was only collecting cans out of desperation. He shook his head; sometimes it was humbling to comprehend so intimately the hardship in other people's lives. When he telephoned his wife that evening he told her, 'I've just had a really strange day. It was bizarre, but sort of heartening.'

'Oh do tell me,' she said.

In Çanakkale, Mehmet dumped his haul of cans by the front door of his apartment, and went into the kitchen to greet his wife. 'I've just had a really strange day,' he told her, 'it was bizarre, but in its way it was quite heartening.'

His wife stirred the wooden spoon in the pot, wiped her hands on a cloth, and said, 'Tell me.'

A NIGHT OFF FOR PRUDENTE DE MORAES

Prudente de Moraes paused briefly to glance down with satisfaction at the freshly gleaming leather of his shoes. He had just had them buffed up by a barefoot and bedraggled fellow with a Bahian accent, paying him more than was strictly necessary, and therefore a feeling of virtue and beneficence was spreading in his stomach as though he had swallowed a fine glass of aquardente with one stylish tip of the chin. It was good to be wearing casual dress, walking as slowly as he liked in the early evening, listening to the crash of the waves and watching the plumes of spray.

He strolled along the Avenida Vieira Souto, dawdling to watch the interminable games of volleyball played by the golden-skinned young men. Just now and then one might see a boy practising fancy tricks with a football and wonder at the elegance and precision of it all. Prudente reflected that often the most beautiful things were those that were intrinsically the most useless.

He stopped at a kiosk and asked for an *agua de coco*, merely for the pleasure of witnessing the attendant ritual, smiling to himself and chinking the change in his pocket as the man delved into his Frigidaire to retrieve a large coconut. He lopped off the end with a machete, so that it would stand on a table if required, and then, with three deft twists of the wrist and three smart blows, he removed a triangle of the outer pith from the other end, through which he inserted a couple of straws. 'The reason,' mused Prudente, 'that he does it with such swiftness and precision, is that he wants me to be impressed. What vain creatures we are.' He took the coconut and sat at the white plastic table, sucking the cold coconut milk into his mouth, and feeling it insinuating its soft liquid tentacles around the contents of his stomach. He had not often had *agua de coco* since he was a little boy, having graduated to beer, but now he resolved to do so more often. Sometimes it was a good idea to reclaim one's past, even if only in the smallest ways. He looked up at the digital clock that had been sponsored by McDonald's, and bathed in the luxurious feeling of having an entire evening to waste.

Prudente decided to take off his shoes and socks, and go down to the edge of the waves. It was a good twenty-eight degrees, but the clouds had prevented the sun from baking the sand directly, and anyway there was a trick to walking on hot sand, which was to keep going and not to think about it.

He wove between the volleyball games, and down to the long flat strip where there seemed to be nobody who was not young and exquisitely beautiful. He felt wistful when he saw the flat stomachs and well-defined pectoral muscles of the young men, and even more wistful when he saw that every one of the young girls was a teenager. Most wore the kind of bikini bottoms known popularly as 'dental floss' because they had no real seat to them, but only an exiguous fillet that disappeared between the cheeks. His eyes roved over hundreds of heartbreakingly brown-buttocked Lolitas laid out in rows on their towels, soaking up the sun, and soaking up the longing of the males who watched them from behind the cool privacy of their sunglasses. It was a beach full of narcissists, he realised, and then reflected with a flash of honesty that the only reason that he himself was not a narcissist these days was that he no longer had very much to be vain about. He watched two men who were floundering comically in the prodigious waves. One was very tall and angular, and the other was short and spherical. Few of the locals were swimming, because the coastguard's red flag was flying, and from their puce faces and eccentric behaviour, Prudente rightly inferred that the two bathers were Englishmen. He watched them being bowled over by the waves every time his eyes needed to be refreshed after having seen yet another fabulous but untouchable girl patrol past him like a panther, or flow by with the loose-limbed elegance of a gazelle.

He was about to leave Ipanema beach when he became aware that a spectacular sunset was developing over the sea by São Conrado. Normally a mist rose on the horizon, obscuring the sunset altogether, but today the clouds and the ocean's vapour had left a space for the sun to display itself, so that it was sinking at a sedate but visible speed, growing ever larger and more splendid. It was incandescent and fluorescent, with a colour that struck him as more artificial than natural. Streaks of vermilion and scarlet spread horizontally, and Prudente wished idly for some orange and black. Orange and black sunsets were his particular favourite, because their savagery made them less sentimental. He loved beauty as much as any man else, but he was not unduly sentimental, and he liked his beauty to be slaked with just a touch of terror.

He realised that the sun was going to sink at precisely the mid-point between the rocks out to sea and the headland, as if it had been aiming deliberately at precisely the most aesthetically pleasing configuration of land and sea. Prudente looked up at the peaks known as 'The Two Brothers', and reflected once again that they looked more like two ill-matched woman's breasts. Come to think of it, the Sugar Loaf was somewhat breast-shaped too. He watched the lights begin to go on in the favela above São Conrado, the pinpricks of light oscillating in the hot air like distant stars. He remembered when the favela had been nothing but sheets of tin and lumps of timber held together with wires and beachcombed lengths of rope. Now they were built of bricks, but they still seemed to disgorge the same plagues of thieves and rogues that they always had.

Prudente did not want to spoil the sunset by ruminating upon intractable social problems, however, and like many others had long ago come to the conclusion that radical cures were required. He turned his attention back to the natural glory of what was happening in the west. The sun was now half drowned, and was throwing out thick and undulating plumes of scarlet fire. They had become like the locks of a woman imagined by an artist who was thinking of a wild goddess, or was attempting to epitomise a passion such as grief, or vengeance, or desire.

Prudente noticed that an odd thing was occurring. The crowds of young Cariocas had risen to their feet, and were facing the west, entranced by the dying moments of the sun. He watched the volleyballers, the footballers, the seekers of suntans, the young heartbreakers of both sexes, the dedicated narcissists who had just become absorbed in something even more beautiful than themselves, and felt profoundly stirred. There must be something naturally wonderful within the human heart, an impulse that opened it to the ineffable, the sublime and the marvellous. He rose to his feet and stood amongst the crowd, sensing sympathetically the waves of unanimous spiritual awe that sparked in the charged air between them.

The sun slipped to the rim of the earth, a final ball of red light flared briefly like a ruby at the outer edge of the sea, and then it was gone. Spontaneously the throng of Cariocas burst into applause, congratulating the sun and the sea upon the finest possible performance, as if the whole world had become a theatre and the human race the spectator to its virtuosity. The sky darkened to violet-blue, but still the people stood silent, as if awaiting a curtain call. A cool gust of wind blew in off the southern Atlantic, and a sigh passed through the crowd. Without a word, Rio de Janeiro's throng of beautiful young sybarites leaned down, picked up their beach paraphernalia and walked quietly away towards the Avenida Vieira Souto. They would take a final Guarana perhaps, a final Coca-Cola, a final *agua de coco* from one of the kiosks, and then be off home before the thieves came down from the slums.

Prudente had been deeply stirred by the whole experience, not merely by the extraordinary splendour of the sunset, but also by the unexpected manner in which it had seized the hearts of so many people simultaneously. Chills had run down his spine, and his own sigh had joined the susurration of the crowd at the final moment of the sun's descent. He would have felt the same if he had caught a glimpse of the Virgin Herself, or seen St Sebastian ride through the city with his incorruptible body full of arrows. He went to a bar in the Rua Visconde de Piraja, and ordered a caipirinha.

He watched the barman crushing the ice by whacking it with a spoon, and observed him slicing the limes, putting in the sugar, and finally pouring the spirit. He took the glass and braced himself for the impact; the first gulp was always a shock to the system, no matter how many times one had drunk it before in one's life. It was that strange combination of sweet, bitter and sour. Prudente never drank more than two at one sitting, because it had a most insidious way of making one drunk; one might suffer double-vision, for example, whilst remaining otherwise clear-headed.

Prudente drank his two caipirinhas over a period of one hour, engaged in conversation with a fat and intoxicated security man who rather tediously insisted upon showing him his pistol, and then wandered out into the night. It was humid, a trickle of sweat began to slip down his temple, and he wiped his mouth with the back of his sleeve. He decided that he would walk down the Rua Garcia D'Avila to the lagoon, so that he could look at the Christ, floodlit at the top of the Corcovado Mountain. It was a sight of which he could never tire, for sometimes the top of the mountain would be enclosed in mist, and the gigantic Christ would glow gold, as if coming in glory upon the clouds at the resurrection of the dead. Equally one could imagine that the Christ was an angel, perhaps Michael or Gabriel, and Prudente wondered how many crimes had been prevented by a thief or a murderer looking up at the last moment, and being reminded of the omnipresence, justice and beauty of God. Sometimes Prudente wondered how anyone could do wrong in Rio, with the Christ resplendent in the sky at night.

Prudente knew that it was foolish to wander these streets unaccompanied, and without urgency or purpose in his stride. He realised with wry honesty that he did not live up to his name at times such as this, and therefore he was not altogether surprised when an arm went around his shoulder, and the barrel of a gun was stuck into his ribs. He knew immediately that he being robbed, but, strangely enough, he also realised that he could not be bothered to be alarmed.

'*Senhor*,' said the robber, walking along with him with his arm around his shoulder in apparent friendship, 'you are richer than me, and I am very poor. If you give me your money and your watch, you will come to no harm.'

'How do you know that I am richer than you?' demanded Prudente, with an edge of irritation in his voice. 'And if you're so poor, how come you can afford to buy a gun?'

'I stole it,' replied the man, offended at the suggestion that he was lying about being poor.

'Then you probably haven't got any bullets, have you?'

'Of course I have bullets.'

'Prove it. Go on, fire into the air or something, and then I'll believe you. Otherwise I give you nothing.'

'If I fire it, everyone will come running.'

'If you don't fire it, I must assume either that you don't have any bullets or that it's a replica.'

The thief sucked his teeth in irritation and poked the gun a little harder into Prudente's ribs. 'Come on, cut the chatter. Hand over.'

Prudente continued both to be calm and to be surprised at how calm he was. He changed tack. 'Do you know how boring you are?'

'Boring?'

'Yes. Very boring. Today I had a day off work, I had my shoes polished, I walked on the beach, I saw a beautiful sunset,

I had a couple of caipirinhas. I was happy, and then you have to come along and disturb my peace of mind when I was only going to have a look at the Christ. It's boring. Look, I'll show you how boring you are.' Prudente reached into his trouser pocket and produced a sheaf of cruzados. 'Have a look at those, I keep them specially for muggers.'

The thief looked down at them and said, 'They're out of date. You can't use cruzados any more.'

'Precisely, but in the dark a thief just takes them and runs, and looks at them later. I've been mugged four times, and now I carry a little wad of cruzados. And look at this …' Prudente reached into his shirt pocket and brought out a rectangle of plastic. 'This is an expired credit card that I carry for the same reason.' He drew himself up to his full height and inhaled as if with exasperation. 'That is how boring you are. You and your kind are so inevitable that I don't even care about it.'

The robber appeared both crestfallen and insulted. He avoided Prudente's reproachful and disdainful glance, and said, 'Nonetheless, hand over the cash, and your watch.'

Prudente held up his left wrist. 'Plastic watch,' he announced, with a glee that was almost malicious, 'resale value nil. What a shame.' There was a long pause as the two men looked at each other, and then Prudente said, 'Are you poor and hungry?'

'Yes. Why else would I do this?'

'Because you're a lazy son of a bitch who won't get a real job? Because you have no sense of morality? Because you like the excitement? Who knows?'

'I am poor and hungry,' insisted the thief.

'You have nice clothes. Nice shoes. A nice gold tooth.'

'Nonetheless, I am poor and hungry. Not everything is as it seems.'

'So you don't like to do bad things?'

Prudente felt the barrel of the gun prod with less intensity into his ribs. 'Of course not,' replied the robber at last.

'Come and have dinner with me,' proposed Prudente. 'I have an evening off, and if you are so hungry, then you can have a free meal on me, without doing anything bad.'

The robber eyed him suspiciously. 'I think I'll just go home,' he said at length.

'No, no, no, come on, I invite you. Be my guest. I'd like the company. What's your favourite meal?'

'Feijoada.'

'Ah, me too, but I don't know anyone who serves it in the evening. By the middle of the afternoon there's nothing left. I'll take you to a churrasco house, perhaps, and we can have a picanha. How about that?'

'What's the catch?' asked the thief, finally putting the gun into the waistband of his trousers.

'We've got to go and look at the Christ first.'

'One false move and I shoot,' warned the thief, who had watched a great many westerns on the television, and had picked up one or two of the most time-honoured clichés.

Together the two men walked down to the lagoon. They saw a row of white egrets perched upon a jetty, recuperating from a hard day's fishing, and one man with a torch was paddling in the shallows, hoping to attract a fish or two to the pool of light that he was casting upon the water. In his right hand he held a machete with which to dispatch his victims. High above, the statue of Christ shone in glory above the clouds, its arms outspread in a gesture that was both a crucifixion and an embrace.

'I come here when I need to think, to have a little consolation,' said Prudente.

'I like it too,' said the thief.

'Where are you from? You don't have a Carioca accent.'

'I'm from Salvador. I love it, but to be honest, there's no future up there. Rio's where the money is.'

'And São Paulo.'

'São Paulo's OK. Brasilia's just one big traffic jam.'

'You're right there. Come on, let's go and eat. We can try Luna's or Paz E Amor.'

'I've never been to a proper restaurant,' said the thief, 'you'll have to tell me what to do.'

In Paz E Amor Prudente watched with satisfaction as his guest chewed enthusiastically upon the medallions of rare beef. Juice trickled down their chins, and they clinked glasses at every gulp. Prudente had chosen first a bottle of Concha y Toro from Chile, and then a bottle of Brazilian Forestier. 'We Brazilians make good wine,' he observed, 'but we've forgotten to tell anyone. All the more for us, eh?'

The dish of picanha was large enough for four people, but the two of them managed to demolish it nonetheless, with the aid of copious draughts of mineral water and swigs of the fine red wine. Prudente instructed his guest upon the art of attracting the waiter's attention and explained that you always get better service if you say 'thank you' a great deal. 'What's your favourite football team?' he asked.

'Flamengo. What's yours?'

'What a coincidence. Mine's Flamengo too. Did you see the game last week?'

'I heard about it. Did you see it?'

'It was fantastic.'

'I heard it was. I couldn't get in, so I went and had a drink.'

Prudente attracted the waiter with a snap of his fingers, and said, 'Two cognacs. Have you got the one with the ginger in it?'

'Macieira, sir?'

'That's the one.'

Prudente showed the thief how to warm the glass in his hands so that the vapour would rise up and be trapped in the glass. He showed him how to sniff it. The thief inhaled deeply, a slow smile spreading across his face. '*Nossa Senhora*! I could get drunk on that alone,' he said.

'Have you heard the rumour about the police executing people like you?' asked Prudente.

'People like me?'

'Thieves, armed robbers, that sort of thing. They say that the cops are so fed up with lawlessness that they're taking the law into their own hands.'

The thief looked at him reproachfully, as though resentful of being named for what he was. 'I heard it was the police who killed all those street children on the steps of the Candelaria.'

'I don't think the police kill children,' said Prudente, 'but I heard they were killing people like you. Somebody found a corpse on the Corcovado recently. Apparently they only do it in their spare time, when they're out of uniform. That's dedication for you, eh?'

The thief regarded him, a small glow of fear alight in his eyes. 'Don't talk like this,' he said, 'it gives me the creeps.'

'Hey, I bought you a meal. You're OK with me. By the way, was I right in thinking that you didn't have any bullets? Too expensive, eh? Or is the gun a replica?'

'I've got bullets,' said the thief, 'I just don't like to kill anyone. It's bad enough when someone like you keeps reminding me that I'm a thief, but I'm not a murderer. I hope I never sink to that.'

They sat in companionable silence, sipping their cognac, and feeling the picanha lie in their stomachs with the mildly uncomfortable weight of a small cannonball. 'I've got to go to the men's,' said the thief, 'keep an eye on my things.'

'That's OK; I've got to make a phone call. Do you want me to order some coffee? Do you like it pure, or with sugar?'

After the thief had gone, Prudente took his mobile phone from his jacket, stabbed at the buttons, and talked for a few moments into the receiver. He put it down as the thief re-appeared, and let it lie on the table, as if to indicate, 'You could have stolen this.'

'Do you mind if I look at your gun?' asked Prudente. 'I have an interest in them.'

'In a restaurant?' protested the thief. 'Certainly not.'

'Oh, go on. Just pass it under the cloth. Take the bullets out first if you want. Is it a nice one?'

'Browning automatic, 9mm. It's a sweetie.'

'Let's have a look.'

The thief thought about it, and then removed the weapon from inside his jacket. He withdrew the ammunition clip and passed the weapon under the tablecloth. Prudente hefted its weight in his hands, and said, 'I prefer a .38 revolver. I mean, with automatics you can't ever be sure that they're not going to jam, and if that happens in a tight spot, you're done for.'

'I know.' The thief leaned forward confidentially. 'I bet you'll never guess where I got it from.'

'You said you'd stolen it.'

'I bought it from one of the soldiers at the Copacabana Fort.'

'*Nossa Senhora!*' exclaimed Prudente. 'I heard that such things happened, but I didn't think it was true.'

'They're all in it,' said the thief bitterly. 'Police, politicians, the army, you name it.'

'I don't know why you're so disgusted,' said Prudente, 'you're a thief yourself.'

The thief looked at him wearily. 'As you keep reminding me.'

Prudente reached inside his jacket and withdrew a pair of panatellas. 'Cigar?' he asked. 'It goes well with the cognac and coffee. A good way to end the evening happily.'

The thief accepted the cigar and blew out his cheeks. 'I'm stuffed,' he said. 'Tomorrow I'll be shitting pure blood, like a vampire.'

The two men watched with interest as a Military Police vehicle disappeared slowly around the corner. 'They're up to something,' observed the thief, 'you can always tell. When the sirens are going, you know that they're just trying to get home quickly. It's when they're creeping about that you know something's up.'

'You're probably right,' said Prudente, nodding his head and blowing a thick cloud of blue aromatic smoke into the air above the thief's head.

'Nice cigar,' said the thief.

'I'm going to pay the bill,' said Prudente de Moraes. 'It's time we were off. It's been a great evening. After an inauspicious start to our acquaintance, I am beginning to feel that I have almost made a friend.'

'You've been very kind,' said the thief, 'a true Christian.' He hung his head, and a choke came into his voice. 'I didn't deserve to be treated so well, after what I tried to do.'

As they walked off together, Prudente put his arm through that of his new friend, and they matched step as they considered the beauty and calm of the evening, 'Did you know,' asked Prudente, 'that in the northern hemisphere they see a completely different set of stars? I've often thought of that as a metaphor for something, but I don't know what.'

'It makes you think,' said the thief, and at that moment the two men became aware that ahead of them, coming towards them, were four very large men walking abreast. 'Better cross the street,' said the thief, 'better be on the safe side.'

'It's too late now,' replied Prudente de Moraes. 'All we can do is look strong and confident, and keep going as if we know exactly what's what.'

'Maybe we should invite them to dinner,' said the thief, with a small and very nervous laugh.

'It's OK,' said Prudente, 'I think I know these characters. Friends of mine.'

'That's a relief. I thought we were done for.'

Prudente called out to the men, who were now within a few paces, 'Hey, Vargas, Francisco, Bartolomeu, Paulo, how's things? Good to see you. What a coincidence. Let me introduce you to my friend.'

They shook hands all round, the thief revealing that his name was Luis Ribeiro.